WHEN DARKNESS COMES

Jealousy and ambition divide a tribe. When the final split occurs the two new communities find they are too small to be self-sufficient, and they nearly starve. It is up to the chief's son and the other children of the tribe, who miss their old friends, to attempt reconciliation. Threatened by raiders from a stronger, more skilful race, the tribe reunites just in time . . .

A remarkable novel by a best-selling author, issued in paperback for the first time.

About the author

Robert Swindells was born in Bradford, West Yorkshire in 1939. He left school at fifteen, and subsequently worked as a proof reader on local papers, joined the RAF as a clerk, and on leaving the RAF had a number of jobs, including printing and engineering. In 1969 he entered college to train as a teacher. While there he wrote his first novel, *When Darkness Comes* as a thesis, and this was published by Hodder and Stoughton in 1973. He continued writing and teaching, but gradually writing took over, and in 1980 he became a full-time writer.

When Darkness Comes

Robert Swindells

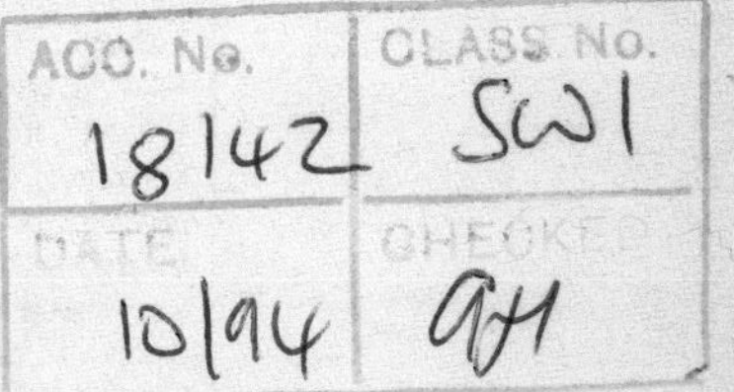

KNIGHT BOOKS
Hodder and Stoughton

For Cathy and the Kids, who lived on chips for me.

First published by Brockhampton Press, 1973

Knight Books edition 1993

British Library C.I.P.

Cataloguing in Publication Data is available from the British Library

ISBN 0 340 58228 6

The characters and situations in this book are entirely imaginary and bear no relation to any real person or actual happenings.

Printed and bound in Great Britain for Hodder and Stoughton Children's Books, a division of Hodder and Stoughton Ltd, Mill Road, Dunton Green, Sevenoaks, Kent TN13 2YA (Editorial Office: 47 Bedford Square, London WC1B 3DP) by Clays Ltd, St Ives plc. Typeset by Hewer Text Composition Services, Edinburgh.

I

Through the golden haze of late afternoon they came; winding slowly between the birches; the big ones laden, strung out, breathing heavily, calling to one another from time to time in short gutturals.

The little ones, brown and naked, flitted lithe over a thickening carpet of thin yellow leaves, black hair swirling; their sharp cries and bubbling laughter carrying far through the deep woodland solitude.

Morg, running lightly, twisted his thin body between the close-crowding trunks, now and then throwing out a long arm for balance; never slackening pace; duplicating every movement of the smaller boy who ran in front of him. As they passed through pools of sunlight and patches of shadow their bodies were honey sometimes, and sometimes burnt oak; and now and then, when they paused, seeking breath or a new way, the long pale autumn rays, shattered by a tree, would stencil a dappled leaf pattern on their glistening backs.

Morg cupped a hand round his mouth and shouted, breathless, 'Gyre! You run like a three-legged elk; when I catch you you shall be skinned and roasted!'

Gyre, hard pressed, turned his head as he ran.

'A poor hunter you must be, given such a run by a three-legged elk!' he cried.

'I run not to catch you, but to tire you!' rejoined Morg. 'When I have tired you, then I will show you speed!'

'When you catch the elk, beware of his horns!' flung back Gyre, as he plunged on, tiring.

Morg, sensing that his comrade was spent, put on a spurt, and, closing to within leaping distance, threw himself forward, his long arms closing round Gyre's knees. Both boys crashed to the ground, flinging a shower of leaves into the air. Laughing, Morg pulled himself on to Gyre's back, and lay on him, pinning his smaller friend helpless to the earth.

'I feel no horns, little elk,' he taunted.

Gyre's wiry body squirmed impotently under Morg's weight, and his voice came gaspingly.

'You think you're a great hunter, because Daf is your father,' he hissed. 'But even Daf cannot match *my* father in hunting prowess – the chief himself cannot. Let me up now, for some day you will ask the same of me!'

Startled by the venom in Gyre's tone, Morg rolled over, releasing him, and made to rise. Fast as an adder, Gyre uncoiled, and his fist took the kneeling Morg in the mouth, drawing blood.

Standing over his still kneeling adversary, fists clenched, Gyre spoke gratingly through bared teeth.

'Everybody thinks that Daf will be our next chief. But Daf is grown gentle with age – he supports the old chief, who is too feeble already to lead us. Soon, both will be swept away. Then we shall see who brings who to the earth!'

Then he whirled, and Morg, too surprised to move, watched as the slight figure jinked swiftly between the slender trees towards the path taken by the tribe. Then he hoisted himself slowly to his feet, wiped the back of a hand across his mouth, and gazed thoughtfully at the smear of blood on the knuckles.

'Yes, Gyre,' he whispered. 'The chief is old, and no longer hunts. But it takes more than skill in the hunt to make a chief!'

He shook his head, and began to make his way, frowning, towards the main party. The cries of the children guided him as he walked.

'Perhaps,' he thought, 'my father should hear of this.'

In the dusk the old chief turned to look at his tired people. He spoke, and his voice was like dry leaves in the wind.

'A little faster, my people. Our journey is nearly done, but the sun also is near his rest.'

With sighs and grunts, the tribesfolk increased their pace a little. Far away a wolf howled, and the chief rapped, 'Call the children to you and keep them close. Daf! Gawl! Take your spears and guard our flanks. Modd! Drop back to the rear, and keep watch at our backs. Let nobody straggle. We cannot pass the night in the forest. The lake is close at hand, where we shall be safe.'

The warrior Modd, rearguard to the tribe, had keen ears, and when Morg came rustling out of the trees, the spear in the hunter's raised hand was pointed at his chest. Morg raised an arm in greeting.

'It is I,' he called. 'Put up your spear!'

Modd, a surly man and a fine warrior, grunted, 'Approach me like a wolf, and one day you will die like one. And salute me not as man to man, but get you forward, with the other children.'

Morg, abashed, passed with lowered head towards the centre of the moving column.

On any other day, the warrior's words would have brought fire to his cheeks, and rebellion to his heart, but now he had other things to think about. His father was guarding a flank, so Morg could not speak with him now. That must wait until they reached the lake. On the other flank, he could see, dimly, the figure of Gawl, father of Gyre, stalking, tensely watchful, through the twilit trees, spear at the ready. No creature of the night, Morg knew, would pass by Gawl unseen. A young man, Gawl, and already the leading hunter of the tribe. Always ready to lead the attack; even, sometimes, when others thought that retreat might be the wiser course. The tales of his battles with wolf, bear, and wild bull were told and retold around the night fires.

Ahead of him Morg saw Ela, the daughter of Trond, bent under her load of skins and cooking-pots. When they were small, Ela and he had been constant companions, running together in the hills; splashing carefree in cool chattering streams. Ela it was who, four summers old, had skinned and cooked Morg's first kill, and, laughing with the exhilaration of their adult-seeming roles, they had shared the half-cooked flesh of the young hare, tearing at it with tiny teeth grown fierce. Since that day, though nothing was ever said, it had been understood between the two of them that Ela would await her man in Morg's lodge some day, when, grown at last, he would lead his companions in the hunt. Morg approached the toiling girl and, grinning, said, 'You are bent as though you carried the sky on your back. Let me take the skins awhile.'

Ela paused and looked at the boy, and there was pain in her eyes.

'No, Morg. You must not walk with me. You and I have separate trails to follow. My father has said that I must tell you this.' The pair gazed at each other for a moment. Ela's eyes brimmed, and there was in Morg's throat a tightness that ought not to afflict the son of a leader. He compressed his lips, jerked his head erect and strode on, unable to speak for fear of the weakness in him which his voice might betray.

Morg remembered his other winters at the lake; happy, peaceful times, in spite of the cold. The men going off to hunt; the women keeping the fires high with wood gathered by the children; his friends and himself, fishing or playing on the ice. Then, in the cold evenings, sitting huddled together near the biggest fire, watching the meat roasting, and listening to stories of the hunt.

Morg screwed his eyes into the gloom, until he made out Gyre, walking some way ahead, very erect, with a small fish-spear on his shoulder. A frown creased Morg's brow. Had Gyre's anger made him shout foolish untruths, or had that anger caused the boy to speak of something he knew, and should have kept silent about? A sense of uneasiness came like the twilight into Morg's mind. Would this winter be like the others? Or would it perhaps bring trouble into their lives?

Somewhere nearby, little Lidi was grizzling softly, tired out at last. The weary straggle of people lurched on, towards the place where, beneath pale stars of evening, a calm lake awaited placidly the first cold winds of winter.

2

The first probing fingers of the unrisen sun smeared pale green streaks low above the horizon, and a sharp breeze hustled the lake mist, teasing it into shreds which slid ghostly up the reedy bank and drifted away between the trees. The shore here consisted of a wide, swampy reed bed which extended to where a slight rise in the terrain provided firmer ground for the birches.

Upon this swamp, a large square platform of criss-crossed birch boughs had been laid. When the thick growth of reeds was rippled by the wind, the platform looked like a huge raft, adrift on a turbulent sea of green. Upon the dry deck of this platform stood seven low huts, made by throwing animal skins over a framework of boughs. These houses seemed poised for imminent collapse; as though the thong-lashed frames could barely support the weight of the skins upon them.

The platform had been here for many years, occupied in the winter months, abandoned each summer, its huts, flayed of their skins, crouching like gaunt skeletons beside the water. Each autumn, when the people returned, they found their platform partly settled into the thick ooze, so that here and there on the deck, shallow depressions had become muddy puddles, the boughs at these points rotten and black. Sometimes, they would find that a hut-frame had collapsed; perhaps in a summer storm, or perhaps pushed over by one of the many animals which came here in the spring, to sniff out food scraps left by the people.

Then, the work of repair would be done. It would occupy many hours, and when it was done the people would be ready to face another winter. This time, though, they had reached their village in the dark, and had been forced to throw skins over swaying frameworks. Tilde, the fire-carrier, had laid her precious flame among a heap of hastily gathered bark and twigs, and, except for Modd, left to tend the fire and to keep a watch, the people had thrown themselves down to sleep, oblivious of their damp floors and precarious roofs.

Now, as dawn approached, Modd, squatting close to the grey ashpile of the fire, raised his shaggy head from his chest, shook it to dispel the mists of fatigue, and, grunting, pushed the tip of his spear into the fire, so that a shower of sparks crackled up and, caught on the breeze, went spinning away across the platform. He had stirred up a shoal of small flames which now he fed with handfuls of dry twigs. The wind gusted, blowing on the embers, so that the hunter's leathery face became suffused with an orange glow. He shuffled his feet as near to the heat as he could, and sat watching the wind-patterns on the grey water.

In his father's hut Gyre lay, sprawled across a scattering of skins on the damp floor. He lay on his stomach; one arm folded beneath him, the other flung out towards the creaking wall, the hand resting lightly on the fish-spear he had carried here in the night. There was a hole in the wall near his head where two skins failed to meet, and the moaning of the wind as it came sighing into the dank interior penetrated the heavy layers of sleep in Gyre's head, so that he grunted, sighed, and slowly opened his aching eyes. He could make out the huddled shape of his mother, dark against the far wall. Her arm was flung limply across the tiny bundle that was Gyre's baby brother, Pab. All this was familiar, yet Gyre felt instinctively that there was something unusual stirring. His wiry body, tuned by constant danger to instantaneous reaction, tensed; his hand tightened round the puny spear.

He lay for a moment, unbreathing, until he identified the exact position of a faint rustling in a dark corner, accompanied by heavy breathing. Then he rolled and came to his knees, his spear arm over his head for a lunge or a throw. He froze.

In the corner crouched three men. The nearest was Gyre's father, Gawl, who now leaned towards the boy, and made urgent signs that he was to be silent, and lie down again. Then he turned back to his two companions, Alpa and Trond, whom Gyre had also recognised. These two, he knew, always stayed close to Gawl when the men hunted. They admired his father's daring, and considered him the finest hunter in the village. Now, as Gyre sank back to the floor, the three began talking in hushed voices.

Several times during the past few days, these three had met briefly, and whispered words had been exchanged. Sometimes it had happened in the evenings, while the people sat at their fires in the summer hills; sometimes they had walked together, a little behind the other men, when they left for a hunt: and once, they had come, as they had now to Gawl's shelter, but this had been in the evening, when the men often visited the shelters of their friends, and there had seemed nothing strange in the meeting – except to Gyre. Gyre had been sitting on the ground, his back against the skin wall outside his father's flimsy summer shelter. The men had approached from another direction, and had not noticed him there. He had heard them go into the hut, but had thought little of it, until he heard Alpa say, in a loud, insistent whisper:

'You *know*, Gawl, that you are the one most fitted to lead us; the chief is old, and he and his followers must be swept away.'

Gyre had got up then and walked softly away; it had been obvious to him that such words are not said to be overheard, by anybody: but he had kept them within himself, turning them over and over in his mind; seeing at length how they tied in with the numerous furtive meetings which had taken place among the three men.

Now, though he strained his ears with all his concentration he could make out nothing that was said. There was only a low murmuring with occasionally a sharp exclamation. What would these three do, he wondered, if they knew that he, Gyre, was already aware of what they were discussing? And further – here a wave of cold dread washed through him – what would they do if they knew how, in anger, he had blurted their intention to Morg? The remembrance of his foolishness yesterday now took possession of his mind, so that he was hardly aware of the three earnest talkers in the gloom. Had Morg told anyone? His father? Perhaps Morg had taken his words as mere boasting; as a way of frightening a stronger adversary. Gyre hoped that this was so. If not, then perhaps the chief and his friend were already aware of the plot which was hatching; and if that were so, then it would go very badly for Gawl and his followers when they came out in the open, expecting the advantage of surprise. They might die; at best, they would be overpowered, and probably banished from the community.

Gyre had a moment of indecision, when he wondered whether it might be best to go to the chief and tell him what was happening. There would be banishment for all the plotters, and their families. But at least the men's lives would be spared.

When he thought about his own life after banishment, though, he shuddered, and rejected this idea. He would be sent away, to live among those he had betrayed. How infinitely better to let things go on; to have the chance to be the son of a chief! In that moment, though they did not know it, the three warriors gained an ambitious young ally.

Across the platform, in the hut of Daf, Morg lay; sleepless. All night he had lain, turning this way and that on the creaking boughs. Gyre's words echoed in his head.

'Soon, both will be swept away. Then we shall see who brings who to the earth.'

The ranting of a furious boy? Words ground out in anger, to deaden a small boy's jealousy and humiliation? Or something more?

He stared at his father's back, where the big man lay heavily near the far wall. He would be thought foolish, running with tales to Daf, about the spiteful bickerings of boys at play. If Daf was to become chief soon, then he, Morg, would be a chief some day too. Was this the way for a future chief to behave – to be frightened into sleeplessness by the words of a child?

He saw in his mind the slight figure, twisting away through the trees; he snorted, shrugged, and turned over.

Then he thought of Old Gart. Gart was by far the oldest of all the people; older, even, than the chief himself. He would have been chief long ago, if he had not had a twisted body since his youth, when he was savaged by the great beast. Now, he sat each day beside his fire, shaping flint points in his gnarled hands, or grinding the red stone for pigment; and at night, with the people close around him in the fire-glow, he would tell over and over stories of long ago; of the days he could recall when the great tusked beast with its shaggy red hair still could be found at its ponderous grazing in the swampy places. His frail body would rock with emotion as he relived ancient hunts, and remembered friends long gone. Gart was old. Gart was wise. Gart would know what to do.

Fastening his garment about him, Morg moved

silently to the low doorway, and emerged, crouching, into the cool dawn.

The huts trailed long shadows across the platform, and Modd, his cold bones aching for the first warmth, watched as the boy trod silently upon the birches; passing the still quiet hut of the chief, and making towards the shelter of Old Gart, which stood at the edge of the water, near to the landing platform where the dugouts lay upside down. Morg did not glance towards Modd, or make any sign, and after gazing after him for a moment, the warrior shrugged and turned back to tending his fire. He was puzzled, in a vague sort of way. There had been much early morning coming and going today; while it was yet barely light, he had seen Alpa and Trond meet beside Trond's shelter; a few muttered words, and the two had moved off towards Gawl's hut. Now Morg was on the move, too. After such a journey as they had come, everybody should have been deep in the sleep of exhaustion: Modd wished he had had the chance to sleep so.

'If I had,' he thought, 'I would not have been creeping around in the dawn.'

He yawned, stretched, and tossed a handful of twigs into the flames.

Morg came near to Old Gart's hut, and paused. Faint, regular breathing was the only sound that reached his ears: the old man was still sleeping. Morg crouched in the entrance, silent, until his eyes adjusted themselves to the gloom, and he could see the ancient warrior, lying twistedly among a pile of skins on the uneven floor. He crawled inside. At Morg's light touch, the old fellow awoke with a start, his hand groping instinctively for a weapon.

'It is I, Morg,' whispered the boy urgently. 'I must speak with you.' Old Gart sat up stiffly, rubbing his eyes with bony fists.

'What?' he yawned. 'What ails you that it must be spoken of at dawn, with an old man, in a fire-less shelter?'

Morg told swiftly the events of the previous day.

'Please advise me, old man,' he concluded. 'Should I tell my father and risk appearing foolish, or keep quiet and hope that I am worrying about nothing?'

Gart was silent for a while. He sat with his hands clasped in his lap and gazed steadily at the boy. Then, in a voice that rattled softly, like dry reeds underfoot, he spoke.

'Some day, Morg, as you have said, you will be chief among our people. When that day comes, you will begin to understand the loneliness of your position: every decision will be yours, in the government of the people, and each decision will carry with it the possibility of disaster. By that time, Morg, Old Gart will have dwelt long among the lost ones. Tell me; to whom will you turn, then, for guidance?'

Morg was silent; his eyes upon the tattered skins before him on the floor. Gart waited. At length the boy looked up into the shrivelled face, and replied: 'When that day comes, old man, I will be my own counsel.'

Old Gart looked at him steadily.

'Then begin now, boy. You will find, when you quietly think about your choices, that you are not *quite* alone. There is something within you which will tell you what you should do: a voice, so small and so distant that, unless you take the time to listen quietly, you will never hear it.'

Morg nodded.

'I will listen, old man,' he said, softly. He made to rise; the old man restrained him with a hand.

'While you are listening, Morg,' he whispered, 'ask this question, silently, in your head. Am I, perhaps, unwise to put my chief and all his people into possible danger, so that I might not make myself appear foolish?'

Morg nodded again, slowly, and got to his feet. Gart's eyes followed him, as he crouched to the doorway.

'And Morg,' the old man called after him, gently. Morg turned. The old eyes smiled a little in the gloom.

'Even the chief asks Old Gart, sometimes.'

Morg, smiling, nodded again and went out.

The sun burnt heavy on the eastern horizon, and rose, sluggishly. Wisps of orange-tinted mist whirled with the breeze across the choppy water. The cooking-fires burned low, as the women scraped the remaining food scraps out of their rough, earthen jars with sticks. When this was done, the three daughters of the village, Ela, Cyl (who was Morg's sister), and tiny Lidi, would carry all the jars to the water's edge, and rinse them out, scrubbing the insides with handfuls of dead reeds. The morning meal was over.

The five hunters met briefly, weapons in hands, before striding off, in single file, towards the dense birch forest. Gyre, sitting near the low fire before his father's hut, watched them go. Daf, as always, was in the lead, his long keen spear ever at the ready, his shrewd eyes alert for possible danger. Gyre's mouth grimaced faintly, but his eyes smiled. He was not sure what was going to happen today, but he knew that something was; and his remembrance of what he had overheard led the boy to suspect that tomorrow, perhaps, he would sit here and see his own father lead the men off into the forest.

'Then,' he thought exultantly, 'then, I shall know what it feels like to be the son of a leader; to know that some day I will be a leader, also. And Morg can watch them go, and know what I have felt all my life – if he lives.'

This last thought sent a surge of hatred through Gyre's breast, so that he repeated the words in his head, 'If he lives'.

Morg was not watching the men. Standing quite still, in the shadow of Daf's hut, the tall youth gazed at Gyre. He did not miss the grimace; the glint in the boy's eyes. Neither was the faint, unconscious movement of Gyre's lips lost to him, though he could not tell what was said. He watched, until the younger boy rose, ducked into his father's hut, and emerged with a fish-spear, with which he walked off with a jaunty air towards the edge of the platform. Then, taking his own fish-spear, Morg moved quietly into the reeds, at a point some distance from the place where Gyre had taken to the marsh.

The footfalls of the five hunters barely disturbed the morning quiet as, in single file, they moved through the trees. Daf, as always, was in the lead. Gawl, Alpa and Trond came behind him, and Modd brought up the rear. They moved quietly, and their long shadows went before them, gliding through the twisted shadows of the trees. A damp smell rose from the ground. Presently, Daf came to a place where a narrow track wound away into the bracken that grew, at this point, thickly between the trees. Here, he stopped. This track was a pig-run; a track taken by wild pigs as they moved in herds from rooting-ground to watering-place, and back again. The other men came up with him, and they spoke together in low voices. Not far from the spot where they stood, they knew, was an open, marshy place, where wild pigs were often to be found feeding. It was towards this place that the pig-run led. Daf motioned to Trond and Alpa.

'Circle quietly until the feeding place is between you and this run. We three will conceal ourselves beside the run. When you are at the right place, move noisily towards the feeding pigs, striking the trees with your spears, and making loud noises with your voices. When the pigs come down the run, we will be waiting with our spears.'

Trond and Alpa hesitated, looking at each other, then at Gawl. Gawl spoke.

'Let me go with them,' he said. 'The greater the noise, the more frightened will be the pigs, and one man on each side of the run is enough to do the killing.'

'Go then,' said Daf. 'And beware the old boar, who might not run from you, but charge you.'

Daf and Modd watched, until the three had slipped away, and then, spears at the ready, they melted noiselessly into the bracken on either side of the run.

Gawl went only far enough into the trees to ensure that Daf and Modd could neither see nor hear him, and then he stopped, and spoke to his two companions.

'Now is the time. Those two will lie in wait for the pigs that never come, and when they return to the platform, it will be ours.' Trond's face wore a worried look, and his hands were restless on his spear-haft.

'I say that we should kill them here in the forest,' he argued. 'Daf will never accept you as chief. He will always be a danger to you.'

Gawl shook his shaggy head.

'No. Daf is liked by the women and children. To kill him would make more enemies. We will hold Morg, and force Daf to accept me as chief before all the people, or to accept banishment. He must serve me, having once sworn to it, for that is our way.'

'Also,' said Alpa, 'we need Modd and Daf to hunt for us, if we are to feast well until the warm time.'

Gawl laughed.

'How good it will feel, to make him follow where he has led all his life.'

'Be wary of him,' warned Trond, 'for he is wise.'

'He is old and grown slow,' sneered Gawl. 'And now, quickly, back to the lake. I grow impatient to see our sickly chief on my spear-point.'

And the three plotters, strung out in single file, ran swiftly between the trees, and their shadows, shorter now, flitted along behind.

The pike oared its lazy way between the reed stems, its striped back blending with the rippling shadows that played along the shallow water. Morg, spear poised, stood heron-like among the reeds, and watched. The tension in his upraised arm caused the ivory point of his spear to tremble slightly, and tiny, sun-shot ripples lapped at his chilled ankles. The long fish cruised closer, seeking food. The boy could see the ugly snout, where the teeth protruded unevenly. An indolent flick of the tail brought the pike to within an arm's length of his feet. Morg lunged. The water erupted, as he followed through, pushing the spear through the fish and into the silt beneath: pinning his victim and holding it, writhing and threshing, to the lakebed. Letting go the shaft with one hand, he groped for the smooth stone axe at his belt and, lifting it again and again, battered the life out of his impaled victim. When the great fish was still, he lifted it, on the spear, clear of the water, and carried it, twitching, to the platform. Squatting beside it, he used his flint knife to disengage the barbed spear-point from the flesh. The point, he noticed, had lost its tip, and would need reshaping. The fish was a good one; long and plump. He laid it beside the two smaller fish he had speared, and glanced along the platform's edge, to where Gyre stood half hidden in the reeds. The boy seemed intent on his fishing, and did not look up. Morg stood, rehung the axe and knife on his belt, and slipped back into the chilled shallows with his damaged spear. The water now was clouded yellow here, because of the pike's struggling, and Morg, crouching in the reeds, moved along the rim of the platform towards where Gyre fished. He stopped when less than a stone's throw from the younger boy, and resumed his vigil; Gyre had not noticed his approach.

The sun climbed the pale sky. Splashes of light danced on the water, and Morg screwed up his aching eyes and turned them landward for rest.

Gawl was on the platform.

Gawl! Morg caught his breath, and sank soundlessly among the reeds. Gawl was in the shadow of Daf's hut, and his spear was in his hand. Morg's mother squatted on the other side of the hut, pounding roots, but it was towards the chief's hut that Gawl was gazing. Before the door of that hut, Tilde was sitting, working on a wolfskin. Gawl was halfway across the space between the two huts, going at a quiet lope, before she saw him. She screamed, and rolled to one side as the hunter lunged at the doorway with his spear.

On the other side of the platform, where Alpa's hut stood, Trond and Alpa appeared, making towards the lodge of Old Gart. As Gawl threw himself at the entrance to the chief's hut, these two entered the hut of the old man, spear-points probing before them. Morg saw Reda, the woman of Alpa, standing horrified beside her hut, both hands to her mouth. Lidi, puzzled, clung to her mother's robe.

Morg, otter-like, moved oily-smooth through the ooze. No ripple marked his path, and he caused no reed to sway. His eyes were on Gyre. Gyre, who now stood, gazing towards the platform, visions of power in his head.

A cry from the chief's hut.

'Now! Now he dies, and Gawl, my father, is chief!'

No. Gawl emerged, and his spear was unblooded. Trond and Alpa, coming into the sunlight, blinked owlishly, and their spears too were clean. Gawl, holding Tilde fiercely, shouted, 'Where is he? Where are they?'

And Morg, creeping closer, rose like a wraith behind Gyre, who was now moving, uncertain, towards the platform. The three hunters stood irresolute, glancing wildly this way and that, and seeing only confused women and placidly staring children. Tilde crouched sobbing by the hut's wall where Gawl had thrown her.

Gyre froze, as something cold and keen settled with a steady pressure on the skin of his neck. Crouching behind, both hands on the spear haft, Morg hissed, 'Drop your spear, and get you on to the platform; but slowly, or you will go to the lost ones today!'

The three plotters whirled as Gyre, prodded by Morg, pulled his feet out of the mud, with a sucking sound, and stepped on to the platform. Morg's spear-point never wavered. Gyre looked afraid into his father's eyes, and saw fear there also.

Morg prodded the boy to within a short distance of the three, who stood now close together, darting nervous glances in all directions, and holding their spears in defensive positions. The women and children had moved close to their own huts; mothers held children fast, to keep them from going too close to the men.

Alpa spoke, urgently.

'We have been tricked. They knew of our plan. Let us take our women and children and go, Gawl, before the others come back.'

'No!' Gawl snapped. 'The others will not return until the sun is in its descent.'

He turned to Morg.

'You cannot stand thus for ever, boy. There are three of us, and none to help you. Put up your spear.'

Morg shook his head.

'Move but one step towards me, and your son will die.'

'Gawl! Let us be gone, for we have failed. Let us keep at least our lives!'

This from Alpa. Gawl snarled.

'Our lives! Who will take our lives? The chief? Old Gart? Where are they? This boy?' He pointed at Morg sneeringly. 'Modd and Daf? They are far away, hunting pigs that are not there! Morg, put up your spear, and show us where the chief is hiding. You will not be harmed if you obey me now!'

Morg was watching the three men closely.

'You will neither come closer, nor try to leave, if you wish Gyre to live.'

He jabbed with his spear, so that Gyre's head jerked forward, and he cried out.

'When our chief shows himself to you, it will be to judge you,' said Morg. His eyes were fixed on Gawl as he said this, and he failed to notice when Trond took two sidelong steps to his left, and stopped. Gawl saw his comrade's move, though, and taunted Morg, to keep his attention.

'You, a mere whelp, thinking to hold at bay three men who hunted while you wailed in your mother's arms, and dribbled bubbles of her milk down your chin!'

Morg, stung, his face reddening, flared: 'Step forward, Gawl, if you doubt the quickness of my spear. Your son has no such doubt.'

The hunter sneered, and made as though to advance. Morg tensed, and Gyre cried out again as the bone tip bit into his neck. Trond moved again, stealthily. Now he was no longer in front of Morg, but well to one side.

'You are a child, a baby,' laughed Gawl. 'Your spear is less quick than your temper. You will die in your first hunt, from acting in haste.'

Morg bit his lip, and grated, 'No, Gawl. That is *your* weakness, that you act in haste, and without thought. If it were not so, you would not now be standing thus, awaiting your fate.'

Trond, moving again to the side, raised his spear to throw. A woman screamed. Morg whirled, saw the throw, flung himself violently to his right. The spear flashed past his shoulder; he crashed to the bough-floor, rolled, and raised his head, to find himself gazing at the spear-tips of Gawl and Alpa. His own weapon lay uselessly out of reach.

'Now, puppy: the chief's hiding-place, and speak quickly,' snarled Gawl.

Morg pulled himself slowly to his feet. The two spears followed his slightest move. He gazed defiantly into the face of Gawl, and said quietly, 'I have no words to give you. Kill me; for I would sooner die than live under your leadership.'

Gyre, smarting from his recent humiliation, had retrieved his fish-spear, and now stepped forward, brandishing the weapon.

'Let *me* ask him, Father,' he hissed. 'I will make him tell *me*.'

Gawl smiled, without mirth.

'Ask him!' he growled.

Gyre advanced, his bone tip pointed at the older boy's chest.

'Now is the time to feel the horns of the little elk,' he grated, 'and to ask his mercy.'

Morg looked into the hate-distorted face before him, and tensed himself. The spears of Gawl and Alpa were sharp in his back. There was no retreat.

Gyre said, 'If you do not answer me, then I will do what I have so long wanted to do to you, Morg. I will see you on the ground, on your knees. And you will ask only to die quickly.' As he spoke, the boy held the point hard against his enemy's chest, and twisted it this way and that. Morg set his teeth, and made no sound.

Trond had picked up his thrown spear, and now stood uneasily nearby, glancing alternately at the silent women by their doorways, and at the forest's edge.

'Gawl!' he said urgently. 'There is not time for this. If we are not in command here very soon, then the other two will return, and we will be lost.'

Gawl nodded.

'You are right, my friend,' he said grimly.

He moved so as to confront Morg. Gyre, reluctantly, stepped aside, and withdrew his spear-point. It was red at its tip, and blood trickled from a small wound in Morg's chest.

Gawl raised his spear, and said, 'This, puppy, is your last chance to save yourself. Tell us where the chief is hiding, or die.'

Morg looked steadily at him. A mixture of hatred and fear showed in the hunter's eyes, and the boy knew that Gawl would kill him now.

There came a half-smothered sob from the direction of Daf's hut, and the boy looked across into the anguished face of his mother, where she stood with Cyl, his sister. Her voice came brokenly.

'Oh, Morg! You are still a boy . . . You do not have to take this upon yourself. Your father would not have you die for his sake, and neither would our chief . . . and yet, I know that you will do that which seems right to you.'

She drew one hand across her tear-stained face. Morg said, 'You know what I must do, my mother. I will tell them nothing.' He was breathing rapidly; there was a drum inside his head, and he felt sick. 'I will tell you nothing,' he gasped, and closed his eyes.

Gawl's arm went back; Alpa, behind Morg, moved to one side. From this range, the spear would go right through.

'No!'

On the very point of his lunge, Gawl heard, and held. Morg, trembling, opened his eyes, blinked the moisture out of them, and turned them in the direction towards which all eyes on the platform were turned.

In the fringe of the forest, two figures moved. Both moved slowly, and one came with an awkward, dragging gait: Old Gart, following his chief into captivity. Morg groaned. Gawl turned instantly back to the boy, his spear steady. Without again turning from Morg, he called to Alpa and Trond, 'Bring them here to me. Quickly!'

The two loped across the platform, to where the old men stood, waiting resignedly. They were marched in at spear-point, Old Gart being urged by vicious jabs of Alpa's spear. When they were near, the chief spoke to Gawl.

'You have what you wanted; release the boy.'

Gawl laughed again; his humourless laugh.

'The boy will be of further use to me, when his father returns,' he said. 'As for you, and that old cripple,' he nodded towards Gart, 'you are of no further use to anybody, and have not been for some time. Now you will die.'

He pointed to the criss-crossed boughs at their feet.

'Kneel,' he ordered.

Slowly, and somehow, with dignity, the chief knelt. His keen gaze was fixed upon Gawl's eyes, and it never wavered. Old Gart sank down, with difficulty, because of his twisted body. The eyes were bright in his brown, withered face, and he looked at Gawl with something resembling pity.

'You are a man of much skill, and little wisdom,' he croaked. 'You will never be a great leader, because you have no respect for the voice of experience, and no regard for the real welfare of the people. You are strong, and you think that this is the same as being right. I am sorry for you; but I am more sorry for these.' He waved a scrawny arm towards the women and children nearby. 'Our people, whom you will lead to their end.'

Gawl only sneered.

'Your last words, old fool. When next we hear your voice, it will be moaning in the trees, when we sit around our fires in the night.'

He turned to Trond and Alpa.

'Make ready!' he snapped.

The two hunters stood behind the kneeling elders, and raised their spears. Morg stiffened, looking desperately towards the forest. Nothing stirred there. He glanced around the platform. The women stood silent; powerless to intervene. Gyre motioned towards him with the fish-spear, his eyes filled with mockery. Gawl was watching his comrades, but his spear remained steady over the boy's heart. Trond and Alpa looked towards their leader, spears poised. Gart and the chief bowed their heads. Gawl allowed a moment to elapse, savouring his moment of triumph: then he nodded.

'Now!'

There came the sickening thud of a spear driven home, followed at once by a scream, long and tearing. Alpa, falling forward across Old Gart, clawed at the haft that protruded rigidly from his side. Trond, his kneeling victim forgotten, whirled to face the armed man bounding towards him, and, recognising Daf, threw down his spear, and held out his empty hands in surrender. Modd, armed now only with an axe, hurled himself at the stunned and motionless Gawl. Gawl, jerking into frenzied action, turned from Morg and advanced his spear to impale the running figure. Morg sprang, his arms closing around the hunter's powerful waist. Caught off balance, Gawl tottered sideways, recovered, and battered with his spear haft at the boy's head. Modd, jinking around the now wavering point, was upon him. Morg rolled clear, felt a sharp, burning pain in his shoulder, and rolled again. The slender fish-spear haft broke off against the boughs beneath him, and he saw through a mist of pain Gyre, a heavy axe raised above his head, teeth exposed in a snarl in the hatred-maddened face. The axe descended. Morg flung himself aside, and Gyre staggered as his blow failed to connect. Lashing out with his foot, Morg caught the smaller boy on the side of the head, and he fell. Morg threw his body across that of the fallen Gyre, pinning him down. The pain in his shoulder made his head swim, and there came into his mind a picture from yesterday: Gyre, squirming on the forest floor, impotent and furious beneath his heavier comrade.

'Comrades no longer,' thought Morg, dimly, 'and no game this time, little elk.'

His right arm seemed useless; he could not feel it. Wriggling atop the wildly threshing boy to keep from being thrown clear, he groped with his other hand for the axe at his belt and, with his remaining strength, brought it down twice on the jerking head beneath him. Gyre subsided, and lay still.

3

The birch boughs creaked as the chief passed back and forward, his arms folded, his face grim. The eyes of his people followed his every move. A weak autumn sunlight fell upon the gathering, which was divided into three groups. One group was made up of Daf's family, Old Gart, and Modd, his woman and their son, little Mow. They sat close together and listened quietly to what the chief was saying. Nearby sat a smaller group consisting of the women of Gawl, Trond and Alpa and their children, Ela, Lidi and baby Pab. The three women huddled together miserably and whispered together anxiously from time to time.

The third group were the prisoners, Gawl, Trond, and Alpa. Gyre lay with them. All were bound with thongs. Gyre's head ached and he wanted to hold it between his hands, but they were lashed behind him and he was lying on them. That hurt, too. He screwed up his eyes to see the towering figure of the old chief and winced at the pain behind them. By now, he reflected bitterly, his father should have been chief here. The old fool who now paced regally before them would have been dead, and so would that smug creature, Morg.

'How I wish,' he said, silently, 'that I had spitted him on my spear when I had the chance.'

Now, he knew, Morg was only waiting his chance to tell the people how he came to know about the plot; to tell how he, Gyre, had betrayed his own father in a fit of rage.

'Then,' he thought, fearfully, 'I might as well be dead, for if I am banished with my father, he will surely kill me himself for my betrayal.'

The chief was coming to that part now.

'. . . And if we had not learned of this plot, then the prisoners here would have killed all who stood in their way, to take over leadership.'

Gawl, from his painful position on the floor, grated: 'How *did* you learn of our plan; at least let us know *that*.'

'Now they will finish me,' thought Gyre.

The chief hesitated and Old Gart spoke from where he sat beside Daf.

'It was I who learned of it,' he said, hoarsely. 'I am old, and it is given to me to know of such things.'

Relief surged through Gyre.

'They're not going to tell,' he breathed.

Gawl growled, 'It is given to you to know nothing, old fool. I believe you not.'

'Guard your tongue, Gawl,' snapped the chief. 'It is foolish in your position to provoke your captors.'

Gawl sneered: 'I care nothing for my captors. Let them kill me, for it is better to die by the spear than to die slowly of hunger from following senile leaders.'

'We shall see who becomes the most hungry this winter,' called out Modd in his gruff voice.

The chief stood and looked gravely down at the prostrate Gawl.

'Modd is right, Gawl,' he said, evenly. 'For this winter, you will indeed lead your own people in the hunt. And perhaps you will learn then that skill and bravery in the field are not enough by themselves.'

He turned, to where the prisoners' families sat.

'Your men have broken our law, and must be banished from our midst according to that law. But you have yourselves done no wrong, and your children, too, are innocent. If any one of you wishes to remain with us, or to leave your child here, you will be permitted to do so.' He rested his gaze upon each of the women in turn. Jodi, the wife of Gawl, gazed back proudly.

'We go with Gawl,' she said, holding her baby in her arms.

Reda, wife of Alpa, said: 'You have wounded my man, and he will need me. Lidi and I go with him.'

'Go where?' piped Lidi, but nobody answered.

Trond's woman, Hila, also indicated that she would go. Beside her sat Ela, whose tearful gaze now and then had been turned towards Morg.

'Mother,' she whispered, 'is it possible that I might be permitted to stay here?'

Hila reached out, and took the girl's hands in her own.

'I know, Ela, why you ask,' she said, gently. 'But Morg is still a boy and cannot claim you. With whom would you lodge and who would hunt for you?'

The girl looked into her mother's face, and remained silent.

'Come. Your place is beside your father,' said Hila.

And Morg, watching the two women covertly, saw Ela's faint nod, and knew that for him, this winter would be a little colder even than winters are wont to be.

The prisoners' hands were loosed, and they scrambled sullenly to their feet. Alpa, holding his injured side, was helped up by Gyre.

'You have until the sun touches the tree tops,' the chief told them. 'Gather together all that you own, and go. If from this day forth any one of you is found on, or near, this platform, he will be killed as though he were a prowling wolf.'

Gawl, rubbing his wrists where the thongs had bitten into them, glowered at the tall figure.

'You will not survive the winter, any of you,' he growled. 'You are left with two men who can hunt, and eight people who cannot. When the snows melt again, I shall be leader of the only people who remain in all the forest.'

'We shall see,' said the chief, quietly, and he moved away.

Alpa, walking painfully, approached Gawl. He spoke slowly, each breath causing him agony.

'We also have only two hunters, Gawl,' he gasped, 'for until my wound is healed, I will be of little use in the forest.'

'Do not fear, Alpa,' muttered his leader. 'We shall survive: but they shall not. Come, let us stand aside a little; I have a plan which will ensure their downfall.'

And the plotters stood in low conversation, while the other members of their party worked frantically: ducking in and out of their huts, and piling up their possessions on the ground outside. When all was assembled, the three women, Jodi, Hila, and Reda, and the girl Ela, divided the heap into four bundles, and tied them with strips of hide, until each had a heavy, but manageable load of skins, cooking-pots, weapons, tools and ornaments to carry upon their backs.

While they worked, the other people of the village watched them, silently. Once, when Lidi trotted with some small item of property close to the hut of Modd, little Mow ran from his mother's side towards her, calling her name. Lidi paused, waiting for her playmate. A man's length separated them when both mothers called, sharply, and almost simultaneously. Both children stopped.

'Lidi, come away!' snapped Reda, bending over her pile of goods. Lidi looked at her mother over her shoulder, then back at Mow, wide-eyed. Mow returned her puzzled stare.

'Mow!' shrilled his mother. 'Do not go near Lidi; come here!' For a moment they remained still, these two who had lived close together from babyhood: who had splashed side by side in the cool shallows, and had mimicked the occupations of their elders under their mothers' unobtrusive eyes through long summer days. They gazed into the blank of each other's eyes. There was no comprehension; something in the tone of each mother's voice transmitted vague shadows of fear to her child. That was all; and though the figure before it remained totally familiar, with its associations of kinship and security, yet each now saw the other in a subtly altered light, so that each backed away one wary step, before turning, abruptly, to run on clumsy legs in opposite directions.

The sun slid slowly down the sky until its pale rim touched the black treetops in the west. Gawl assembled his band.

'Let us be gone, for we have to go before we sleep.'

He felt his new authority, and held himself erect.

'Walk proudly,' he shouted, defiant of all the eyes that watched. 'For we are the new lords of the forest.'

The women stooped to their bundles, lifting them on strong backs. Ela had, besides her bundle, a glowing brand of reeds, birch bark and resin; she would carry fire to the new home of the rebels. Trond stood beside the stricken Alpa, to assist him. Gawl, spear at the ready, took the lead, and the party moved off. Gyre, acting rearguard to the party, stepped off the platform last, and turning, sought among the silent, watching figures behind him until he found the figure of Morg, and having found his enemy, made a defiant, derisive gesture with his spear. Morg's eyes were following the heavily laden Ela, and he did not even notice Gyre's gesture. She did not look back, but followed her mother, slowly, out of sight among the trees.

And as the sun dipped below the distant tree line, the new lords of the forest lurched away between the near-naked birches. When all sight of them was lost, the chief turned to face his depleted band.

'My people,' he said, gravely, 'this is a bad thing which has befallen us. Gawl is a rash and hasty man, but what he said of us was right; there are not enough hunters among us. We must talk now, and try to find how best we might overcome our difficulties.'

He led the way to the open space at the centre of the platform, where the fire was always lit at evening.

'Tilde!' called the chief.

The woman stepped forward.

'Bring fire, Tilde,' he said.

The people arranged themselves round the heap of dry reeds, sticks and thick birch logs which awaited the flame, and sat, hugging their knees, and gazing without seeing at the ground before them. Nobody spoke. It was strangely quiet on the platform, and there seemed to be too much space. Morg was uncomfortably aware of the skeletons of the three abandoned huts, stripped of their skins, which crouched forlorn near the edge of the platform. He was aware also of the spaces between himself and his father, who sat on his one side, and his sister Cyl, who sat on the other. Usually, when all the people gathered at evening round the fire, there was no space between a person and his neighbour; everybody touched, huddling together for warmth. Now the cool wind passed between the subdued figures, and rustled the dead reeds in the fire heap. The chief stood, arms folded, looking vaguely into the distance across the lake. Darkness was already a spreading stain low in the eastern sky, and the ruffled water was dark there, under the far shore. Tilde came, kneeling with her crackling brand, and touched with it the flakes of dry bark at the fire's heart. A sputtering, and the pungent smell of burning resin on the wind. As the glow flickered, caught and spread, somebody sighed in the twilight, and everybody shuffled a little closer.

Somehow, the bright, smoky glow was comforting; the wavering shadows it conjured seemed to fill the empty places at the fireside, and the emptiness inside each of the people was filled with its warmth. Morg watched Tilde as she withdrew her charred brand. Tilde, the fire-carrier; the bringer of warmth, and comfort, and safety. He saw again in his mind Ela and her tiny flame bobbing away into the flaming sun. Somewhere out there in the gloom, another fire would glow tonight. The boy turned his shaggy head, peering out across the ghostly swamp towards the mist-haunted trees. There came over him a strange, painful feeling. Every night of his life, until this night, the light from one fire had fallen upon all the people: kinship, and loyalty, safety, and belonging; the whole world of the people had been enclosed within the one, big round glow, and everything outside that glow had been hostile. And the men had recounted together the stories of the hunt, and Old Gart had told tales of long ago, and the world behind their chilled backs had melted away; and there had been no need to think about anything outside the fire glow, until tomorrow.

And now, as he curled close to the warmth, the unfriendly vastness behind him would not go away. There was a tale he had heard, once, from Old Gart; a tale about a time, long ago, when it was said that there were other people in the forest. People not of the village. People who were seldom seen, who lived in another village, far away. Who spoke with unknown words. The people had smiled at this tale, for throughout all their summer wanderings, in the hills and through the forests, by lakeside, and along the swampy banks of rivers; wherever they had wandered, never had they seen another man. Never had they found a hut, or a broken pot, or an old, cold fire. No voices had ever echoed through the trees except their own voices. There were no other men. There were only animals, and birds, and, in the night, the lost ones, who cannot approach the fire. The people were happy in this knowledge: for all the other creatures of the forest, be they large or small, were slow of wit, and no match for the cunning ways, the keen spears of the people. Only the lost ones could equal the people in cunning; and they were afraid of fire, and of the day.

Morg shivered, involuntarily. Now there was man, out there in the darkness. There was cunning to match cunning, and the spear to oppose the spear. There was hatred, and greed, and ambition. There were familiar faces, and feelings of warmth; remembrance of shared experience, and knowledge of common humanity. There were helpless little children. And there was the thing which had come between them, to make the people out there in some way different from the people here within the firelight. All of this Morg felt dimly, like something seen through mist in the densest part of the forest. He did not quite know why, but he felt that in some way, whatever befell the divided people in the time to come, living would never be quite the same after this night. A weight oppressed his mind and he frowned, and in his eyes there was a far-away look, as he turned back towards the fire.

The chief spoke for a long time. Now and then, there were grunts of assent from one or another of his people.

Only the children remained silent: Cyl, ten summers old, hugging Mow of the four summers to keep him content, and Morg, who felt himself mature, and was apt to resent the fact that only silence was expected of him still, when important matters were talked of. This night, though, his head was busy with its own thoughts, and it was with a slight jerk that he came back to immediate matters, when he heard his own name mentioned. The speaker was Modd.

'I know that according to the custom of the people, a boy must kill his bear before he may join the hunt, and be regarded as a man. But we are in great need of hunters, and Morg is grown big and strong for his years. Let him join the hunt.'

Morg gasped. A wave of pride swept over him. He was not due to hunt his bear for two summers yet. Silently, he willed his hesitant chief, 'Say yes: oh, please say yes!'

The chief regarded the boy gravely for a long moment, before speaking.

'Morg might hunt; he is perhaps grown strong enough for that: but a hunter has the right to speak in the council. Are we to consider him wise enough for *that*?'

'No! Not the council.' This in the crackly voice of Old Gart.

The chief turned his eyes on the broken old warrior. 'He will be, then, but half a man; hunting, but remaining silent at the council fire,' he said.

Old Gart gazed at Morg; the old eyes fastening and holding the boy's eyes, until Morg felt the flush of his cheeks.

'Let him then be regarded as half a hunter, and half wise, until he has proved himself to be otherwise,' he rattled.

Morg, his face burning, felt a stab of anger in his breast. Was the old man mocking him? He stared back steadily into the battered brown face with its web of dry wrinkles. Then he thought he saw Old Gart smile faintly, and nod his head in self-agreement, as though pleased with his own advice, and it came to the boy that the ancient hunter must have great confidence in him, to advise his chief thus. He allowed himself to smile back, fleetingly, before lowering his eyes.

'Rise, Morg, and step forward.' The chief's voice was commanding. Morg, his thoughts whirling, scrambled to his feet and approached the tall, robed figure on unsteady legs. The chief turned and said something to Tilde, who slipped out of the firelight, and returned carrying a spear which she handed to the chief. Morg stood before him, looking up into the wise, weather-beaten face.

'From this night, Morg, son of Daf, you are a hunter for your people,' the chief said solemnly. 'Take this spear, and use it with skill, for upon this depends your own life, and the lives of those you must feed.'

The spear was put into his hand. It was a heavy hunting spear, with a long point of flint, keen enough to pierce a bear's hide, and big enough to inflict a fatal wound. It was the kind of weapon he had longed to wield since he was as small as little Mow. The kind of spear he had pretended his light fish-spear was, when he had played at hunting with Gyre. He gripped its thick strong haft in his moist palm. He could feel the eyes of all the people upon him in the flickering firelight. He looked steadily into the grave face before him.

'I will use this spear with a strong arm and with a keen eye, in the service of my people,' he said.

Then he was walking back to his place, conscious of the spear's weight, and of trying to walk like a hunter. Mow's eyes regarded the boy with awe as he seated himself beside Cyl. The spear rested across his knees, and the child reached out a chubby hand to stroke the cold smooth point, until Cyl, noticing this, took the hand in hers, and gently pulled it away from the keen edge. Out of the corner of her eye, she regarded the grave face of her brother and smiled a little, her pride showing in the smile. And Morg saw, and though his face remained grave, he smiled deep inside also. Though much more was discussed that night before the fire burned low, and the people dispersed to their huts to sleep, Morg heard hardly any of it. He lay, late that night, on the floor of Daf's hut, with the long spear beside him, and thought dreamily of tomorrow. There was to be an expedition by the men to collect raw flint from the cliff at the far end of the lake. He, Morg, would take his place with the other hunters in the long dugout, and man one of the paddles. He would take his spear with him. Perhaps there would be danger . . . wolves . . . a bear . . . And, smiling at the possibilities, Morg drifted into sleep.

4

The breeze came in at dawn with a trace of frost on its breath, and on the platform, the people were already astir. Tilde, her soft robe close about her, knelt at her cooking-fire. The smell of food moved in the cold air, as Modd, Daf and Morg emerged from their huts, and walked together down to the landing-stage to prepare their dugout. They carried digging-sticks fashioned from antlers, crude wooden paddles and an assortment of small implements. Morg carried his spear. The long canoe which lay upside down near the platform's rim was quickly rolled over and pushed into the water. A stout thong prevented it from drifting away from the landing. Then the three proceeded to load their equipment into it, as it wallowed sluggishly on the choppy lake. It was a clumsy craft, roughly hacked out of one huge trunk, and blackened with age. Here and there along its length it had split, from being saturated, dried out in the sun, and exposed to winter frosts for many years. These splits had been caulked with a mixture of dry reeds and sticky resin and frequently needed to be repatched. This time, however, although the craft lay low in the water, no water seeped through, and the gear was soon stowed. Then, talking together in low voices, the three hunters turned, and made their way back through the early light to where the women worked over their fires. Morg and Daf squatted by the smoky mound near their hut, while the boy's mother stirred the mixture of meat and roots which bubbled in the blackened pot among the flames. Morg was hungry and the food smelled good. Cyl, squatting beside her mother, fed the fire with twigs and flakes of resinous bark until the food was cooked. Then the rough pot was lifted off the fire, and the family sat close around it where it sizzled on the damp bough floor and dipped their hard brown fingers into the steaming mixture. Daf, eyes twinkling, looked through the steam at his son.

'Why do you take the spear to the flint digging?' he asked. 'We go to hunt stone, not bears.'

Morg coloured, and he answered: 'Perhaps there is a bear who will hunt *us* today, Father, or a wolfpack. A hunter should, I think, be always ready.'

Daf nodded, serious.

'You are right, my son,' he said, gravely. 'Perhaps today you will be the one to save us all.'

The old warrior's wife looked at her man reproachfully.

'Do not mock the lad,' she said. 'He has known so few summers, and yet is to be a hunter at your side. Proud you should be.'

Daf saw the brimming of the woman's eyes.

'Fear not, woman,' he said, gruffly. 'We shall be watching him, and no harm shall come to the boy.'

Morg reddened with indignation.

'And I shall be watching *you* lest any harm come to you,' he told the greying warrior.

Cyl laughed behind her hand at his impudence. Her brother had always thought himself a man. Daf regarded his son, gently.

'In your mother's eyes, son,' he said, 'you are yet a child, and will be, to her, long after you kill your bear and live in your own lodge. It is the way of mothers. You can prove to the people your manhood, but you will be for ever her child.'

Morg smiled at his mother.

'I shall be careful, Mother,' he promised. 'And when we have gathered flint, and made points, then I will show you how well Morg the hunter can hunt.'

He saw Cyl's mocking eyes.

'And you, little sister, shall have the skin of my first wolf for a robe!' he told her.

The girl laughed.

'I shall spend a cold winter, if I wait for *that*!' she said, and rolled sideways to avoid his slap.

The meal was over, the three hunters rose and walked down to their clumsy craft. Near the landing, Morg saw little Mow. The child stood near the water's edge, facing inland, and the sun, which was pulling itself sluggishly above the rim of the lake, cast his shadow enormous across the platform. Mow was watching this shadow and striking various fierce attitudes. He was a giant and the tiny fish-spear in his hand looked like a tree trunk. He was too absorbed to notice Morg watching him, and started when the lad spoke close beside him.

'Mow,' he said, solemnly, 'we go to dig flint and will be gone until dark. You will be the only man left to take care of the women, and the old ones. See that you stay alert, and keep your spear always by you.'

'Yes, Morg, I will,' promised Mow, confidently. 'Last night, I heard a bear in the forest, and if he comes near today, I will kill him.'

Morg grinned.

'I am sure that you will, Mow,' he said.

The long canoe, with its three passengers, thrust its blunt nose out into the cold water, and moved slowly away. The people stood by the gurgling landing and watched it go. Old Gart standing crookedly beside the water whispered dryly to his chief.

'If they were not to return, my friend, then we would be seven and not a hunter among us.'

The chief nodded. The peril of their situation had given him a restless night.

'They must return, old man,' he said, 'and with enough flint to last the winter. Soon the earth will be too hard to dig into and we will need many weapons this winter.'

'And in the meantime,' reflected Old Gart, 'let us hope that no enemy visits us here. I am too broken and you grown too old to fight wolves and bears.'

The chief watched his people returning to their tasks.

'Yes. We are quite helpless today.'

He sighed, and felt a small tug at his robe. Both ancients looked down into Mow's earnest face.

'I am to guard the village today,' the child informed

them. 'Stay close to your huts, for last night I heard a bear.'

The old men looked at each other and Old Gart nodded solemnly.

'We shall stay close, Mow,' he rattled. 'And if I were you I would keep watch from beside your father's lodge. It is near the centre of the village, and you can see everything from there.'

The infant nodded, gripped his fragile spear, and marched across the boughs, his tangled black head held high, and his long shadow marching before him. Standing beside his father's hut he wished, with a sudden pang, that Lidi was here to see him.

'Trond!' The sharp call rang out through the morning stillness. 'Trond!'

Gyre sat up, shaking the mists of sleep from behind his eyes. His head ached. Yesterday's events came back and he felt ill. The shelter in which he lay had been hastily erected and its exposed position on the high ground made it cold and draughty. The loose skins flapped in the wind. Gyre groaned.

'Trond!'

His father's voice came again sharply from outside. Gyre crawled across to the doorway and stuck his head out. Against the creaking wall sat his mother. Pab fed happily at her breast. His father stood on the cliff top looking westward over the lake, and called from time to time towards one of the other rickety huts which stood in the long, wind-whipped grass. Presently the tangled head of Trond appeared, and the sleepy hunter emerged grunting, and trudged up the cliff top clutching his robe close about his chilled body. The two men stood talking, and Gyre sauntered up to join them.

'Gyre,' his father addressed him, 'since Alpa is wounded and cannot be with us today, you can join us in something we have to do.'

Gyre nodded.

'Are we to hunt?' he asked hopefully.

Gawl laughed unpleasantly.

'Hunt! Yes we are to hunt, Gyre. We are to hunt something which will come over the waters from there.'

His arm pointed westward. Gyre frowned, puzzled for a moment. Then his brow cleared.

'The people!' he gasped.

'Yes, the people,' Gawl said it with a sneer. Trond sniggered.

'But why will they come here?' asked Gyre. 'How do you know they will come?'

Gawl drew the boy to the very edge of the cliff and pointed downwards. From the base of the sheer cliff a narrow rock-strewn beach ran down to the water. The cliff face was scarred and pitted where the rocks had been torn away and had rolled down on to the beach. Gyre understood.

'Flint! This is where the men come to dig flint.'

'Yes. And soon will come the frost and this cliff will become hard as flint itself. They must come soon and I think they will come today.'

There came a scrabbling sound on the precipitous cliff to their right, and Reda appeared, gasping and dishevelled. She carried water in a skin slung across her shoulders. Gaining the top she paused and called to Gawl.

'A fine place you have chosen for our camp! We must climb cliffs every time we need water!' and she gasped.

Gawl frowned, displeased, and called back roughly, 'Go about your work, woman and do not question my decisions. There are good enough reasons for them.'

'Aye!' flung back Reda. 'I know the reasons well enough, for I know what place this is. But killing men will not feed our children, nor bring us water when the cliff is treacherous with ice!' Gawl only growled at her and turned his back.

The woman lurched off with her water to tend her injured man.

Trond spoke.

'You are wise, Gawl,' he grinned, cruelly. 'When the men do not return, or return without flint, then the people will die from hunger, and we will indeed be the lords of the forest.'

Gawl smirked, hugely pleased by the praise.

'Be loyal to me,' he boasted, 'and you will know no hungry days. We shall hunt and feast and revel at our fires, until winter is gone. Then we shall be lords in the summer hills and when winter comes again, the platform will be ours. Only the bones of the people will be there, picked clean by the wolves, and polished by the wind.'

Down by Reda's hut, Lidi stirred the pot on her mother's fire, and thought about Mow. He would be eating now and afterwards he would have to play alone. Her fat little arm went round and round in the smoke as she swirled the soup with a stick. She hoped that soon this strange interlude would be over so that they could all go back to the others. Her mother was acting strangely. Everybody was. And her father was hurt and it seemed to Lidi that one of the men had done it to him. But men do not, she knew, throw spears at other men. She frowned, shook her head to dismiss the disturbing thoughts and crooned softly to herself, rocking, as the soup went round and round.

Ela was cooking too, and her mind also was somewhere else. She had recognised this place last night, and was worried, guessing what was in Gawl's mind. She watched the two men and the thin boy moving about on the cliff edge. Did they mean to kill those who would come for flint, or only to drive them away and deny them access to the precious rock? And would Morg be with the party in the canoe, when it came? She was torn between wanting to see him and wishing him far away from danger. Perhaps he would be left behind to guard the platform. Her mother came out of the hut.

'Stir the pot, girl; the food will burn!' she admonished, and Ela, jerked back to reality, stirred mechanically.

The sun rose above the forest. The wind gusted up the slope, swooped over the lip of the cliff, and blew down across the lake. The outcasts ate. Gawl and Trond muttered together. Reda went into her hut to feed Alpa. Pab grizzled in his mother's lap. He was cold.

'This is a cold place to live,' thought Jodi, cuddling the baby. Gyre ate little, because of his excitement. Perhaps Morg would come today, he thought. He pictured the figure of his enemy, small at the foot of the cliff, and himself, on the high rim, with his spear at the ready, and he grinned round the steaming root that he gnawed. His mother on the other side of the pot threw a skin bottle at his feet.

'Fetch water, Gyre,' she commanded, breaking his pleasant dream. The boy frowned and hesitated, but Jodi was a powerful woman, and he got to his feet and went up the slope with the skin.

'I am practically a hunter,' he grumbled to himself, 'and I am sent like a girl to carry water.'

He walked along the rim seeking the place where Reda had descended. He came to it and began scrambling down the steep face, which here was just gradual enough to allow a precarious footing. A pebble rolled from under his naked foot and went bounding down to the beach. He watched it go, then, raising his eyes to the bright lake, he froze. Out there, where the far low shore showed hazy on the horizon, something was stirring. A black shape, tiny with distance, and indistinct against the still dark western sky. But Gyre knew that it could only be the dugout from the platform. Turning gingerly, he began to scrabble upward again, steadying himself with his hands. At the rim he shouted, running downhill towards the huts. Gawl heard, saw the boy running down and came to his feet, calling sharply to Trond.

'They come; the canoe is coming!' called Gyre, skidding to a stop in front of his father.

'Very well,' said Gawl, calmly. 'We are ready for them.'

They were standing near Alpa's lodge, and within,

the wounded man heard what was said. He shook his head slowly in the gloom.

'Ah no, Gawl,' he said silently, 'we were not ready for them, for you had posted no lookout.'

The stricken man sighed to himself. He had had much time to lie and ponder during the past night while the pain of his wound kept sleep away, and he was beginning to see that perhaps his admired leader had not all the qualities of leadership after all. Gawl had led them here, to this cold and waterless site, in order to further his plan of revenge. He now meant to kill those whom he had refused to kill yesterday in the forest, when he might have done so more easily. He was brave. He was impetuous. He enjoyed the admiration of others. He was ambitious for his son. He was a mighty hunter. But was he not sometimes vain and stubborn and rather foolish?

'Well,' thought Alpa, 'I threw in my lot with him, and here I am; wounded for him and dependent on him; it is too late now for such thoughts.'

And he sighed again, and turned his face to the wall.

Trond and Gawl hung themselves with weapons. Each had a spear, an axe, and a knife. Trond had his bow also, and a bunch of flint-tipped arrows. Gyre carried his fish-spear in one hand and a sling-shot in the other. Gawl spoke.

'We will lie low until they have beached the dugout, and are right beneath the cliff. Then we will attack with spears, arrows, and stones. We will not go down the cliff, to fight at close quarters. Our axes and knives are to be used only if they manage to climb up to us.'

'How many do you expect?' asked Trond.

Gawl shrugged.

'There can be no more than three,' he said, 'even if Morg is with them. And he may not be with them.'

Gyre's eyes glittered fiercely.

'I hope that he *is* with them,' he grated.

'If he is, my son, then let your aim be true, for he is the cause of our exile,' growled Gawl.

The three went up the slope, dropping on to all fours near the top, to avoid being silhouetted against the eastern sky. They raised their heads cautiously, and peered over the rim. The canoe was still some distance off, but now they could count the three figures in it, and the faint sound of the paddles was audible above the keening of the wind.

'Morg!' breathed Gyre, lowering his cheek into the coarse grass. 'Come, Morg; closer, even closer.'

He closed his eyes, feeling the keenness of his spear-point against his cheek. The three lay motionless, their black hair blowing to and fro with the grasses, and listened. The splashing of the paddles grew nearer, and soon, the men's voices could be made out as they talked together, oblivious of their danger. There came the grating sound of the boat's bottom running on shingle, and grunts as the crew leapt out, and began to pull the dugout clear of the water. Gawl raised his head, very slowly. Daf and Morg, unloading tools from the beached canoe. Modd, spear in hand, scanning the beach and cliff with cautious eyes. Gawl dropped his head, and those keen eyes swept over and passed on. The three were coming up the beach. The sound of tools being thrown down. Muttered words in Modd's familiar tones.

'Let us begin here . . .'

And the thud of an antler pick in the cliff face, five man's lengths beneath. Gawl tapped each of his companions on the shoulder and motioned them forward, till they could look over and down. The men below had discarded their robes, and despite the morning chill, their brown bodies glistened as they worked, chopping, thrusting and levering to get the precious flint out of the chalky cliff. Their spears lay with their robes, discarded. Gawl made a hand signal. Trond fitted an arrow to his bow. Gyre's ivory point was poised vertical above the toiling Morg. Now! At the bow's twang, instinct slammed all three diggers tight in the face. The arrow plucked hairs from Daf's head, and rattled among the rocks. The fish-spear cut a furrow in Morg's shoulder and another in his heel. Modd, struck a glancing blow by Gawl's spear haft, sank to his knees, dazed, and Trond's second arrow transfixed his calf. Gyre's slingshot whirled, humming, but the boy could not bring it to bear. There was a slight overhang, and Morg and Daf were barely visible, pressed to the face. He aimed and loosed at the stricken Modd, still kneeling. The stone cracked into the hunter's jaw, and he toppled over sideways, and lay still. The three on the cliff top were on their feet, whooping and screeching their triumph. Daf made a dash for his spear. A near miss from Trond drove him back to the cliff. He turned his face to Morg, cheek pressed to the chalk.

'Go for the spears. I will draw their weapons,' he

gasped. Then he spun and launched himself outward, jinking between the boulders down the beach. An arrow clattered at his heels and a smooth pebble hummed by his cheek. He glanced quickly back. Morg was under the cliff, two spears in his hand. Daf doubled back, zigzagging, gasping for breath. Whoops from above. Silhouettes dancing. Another arrow, by his head. A final spurt. The cliff. Sweat soaking into rough chalk. He extended his arm to his son.

'A spear!' he gasped.

The haft, cool in his hot hand. A sign to Morg. Make no sound. Like hunting hinds. Both silent, eyes cast upward, tense. Silence. Then muttered words above and a pebble, rattling down. Silence. More muttering. An arrow, exploring, quivering in the sand. Silence, and no motion. Ah! There, vertically above Daf's wet brow; above the wise, salt-stung eyes; a silhouette, outward-leaning in dangerous curiosity. Daf, tense, coiled adder-like, the spear-point quivering, sank slowly, smoothly, into a tight crouch. Black figure against the sky. Lean a little further. Just a little . . . Now! Daf uncoiled, and the spear flashed upward. A scream and the silhouette toppled and came down, jerking, to hit the sand. Gyre.

'Morg – the boat!'

Daf, crabbing along the cliff face towards the fallen Modd. Dragging out and down the beach, the unfeeling heels furrowing the sand. Morg, jinking, gained the boat, pushed it, heavy, down till its blunt stern lifted on the wavelets, lapping.

On the cliff, Trond, desperate, grappling with Gawl.

'No! Do not go down. They will kill you.'

A blow, and Gawl was free, running.

'Gawl! No! No!'

Trond, a silhouette, dancing. And Gawl, coming like a small avalanche down the crumbly water-route to the sand, to his son. Daf, dragging Modd into the shallows, glanced up and saw the crouched figure coming along the cliff; doubled, but clearly seen against the chalk.

'Morg! Take Modd!'

The boy lifted the unconscious warrior, bundling him into the wallowing craft. And Daf, stooping to scoop up stones, ran back up the beach, shouting. Gawl, dragging the boy, backed along the cliff, snarling defiance at his advancing foe, as stones swished round his head. From above, another arrow, thudding into the sand. Daf paused, hurled a last stone upward at the prancing Trond, then whirled and bounded down into the shallows where Morg held the boat, rocking gently. The boy was gazing back at the cliff, to where, a little to one side of the scene of battle, another silhouette was standing. A slight silhouette, that raised its arm, briefly, then melted back below the shoulder of the cliff.

'Go!' Daf yelled, pushing off, and grabbing for a paddle. A boiling of foam, and the clumsy craft surged outwards. An arrow bounced sharply off the prow, and skidded over the lake's surface, hissing. Trond cursed, fitted another and saw it fall short. Beyond range. He dropped the weapon and descended to his leader, who crouched over his son at the cliff's foot. The boy lay moaning, and blood stained the sand from the wound in his armpit from which Gawl had plucked the spear. Trond stood looking down at the pair.

'Not a good hunt,' he said.

Gawl glanced up sharply.

'They did not get what they came for,' he snapped.

Trond said no more aloud, but a voice inside him said, 'They got Gyre, and they would have got you also, Gawl, if I had not stayed at my post.'

They laid hold of the boy, and carried him gently up the steep pathway.

Mow, keeping his vigil still at midday under his mother's vigilant eye, saw the canoe first.

'They come!' he piped. 'The men return!'

And he scampered down to the landing, followed, one by one, by all of the people. Old Gart came last of all, with the chief.

'They return early,' he croaked.

The chief's old eyes peered out across the water.

'Aye; and only two men paddle,' he said tersely.

The old craft bumped the landing and willing hands helped the now conscious Modd out of the bottom. He was not seriously hurt, and hobbled off with his woman towards their hut, with the arrow still protruding from his leg. Mow followed, watching the bright feather of the arrowshaft bobbing up and down as his father walked. Daf was in earnest conversation with the chief, and Old Gart hobbled over to where Morg stood, gazing out over the lake. The cliff was a grey smudge on the horizon.

'You saw her?' the old man rattled.

'She saw me running away,' Morg replied, glumly.

'She saw you wisely retreating,' contradicted Old Gart. 'That is something quite different, and if her new leader had the wisdom to see the difference, he might not be where he is today.'

Morg was not to be consoled. He looked bitterly towards the east again, then turned away.

'I lost my spear,' he said.

5

The last of autumn's leaves, torn from their moorings by the east wind, fluttered to the ground and the forest took on a stark, skeletal appearance. Sometimes, in the mornings, the sparse grasses on the cliff top were fringed with a delicate tracery of hoar, and rattled a little when the wind moved them.

At night, the moon hung like a cold lamp in a bottomless blackness, and it seemed that the silvery, brittle tree-forms of the moon forest might melt like the hoar at the first flush of the sun.

Lidi's tousled head emerged through the doorway. She yawned a white plume which drifted away, melting, and stood up unsteadily; not as yet entirely emerged from sleep. The cliff settlement lay awash in a frigid pink dawn, and woodfire smoke, pink-white, rolled sluggishly away over the cat-ice lake.

The child shivered, and pulled the fox-robe closer; squatted by the fire where her mother cooked, sullen, stirring the pot with a stick.

'Cold,' said Lidi, staring into the embers.

Reda looked at the small figure, slight in its wrapping

of fur; the white naked feet; blue-tinged fingers. Tangled black hair.

'It is cold here,' she muttered through set teeth. 'We sit here to guard the flint, and it is too cold to dig flint anyway.'

Lidi was silent. She knew nothing of the flint, nor the reasons for the people's being here. She knew only that day and night, she had never been so cold. Reda stabbed into the pot, and pulled out a chunk of hare, steaming on the stick, and held it out for Lidi.

The little girl ate hungrily, clutching the hot flesh with both fists so that the juices ran up her soft forearms. Here was warmth, to fill the dull ache inside. She looked around, chewing. Trond was working at his hut, piling extra skins on top of it, and inspecting carefully around the walls for holes. His woman Hila was eating by her fire and Ela sat near her mother, working at a wolfskin.

In the doorway of Gawl's lodge, Jodi sat suckling Pab. Lidi regarded Pab, almost spherical in his layers of furs. Pab would not be cold. Lidi shivered, vaguely envious of the infant. Down the slope, by the first trees, Gyre was throwing spears at a bole. Gawl was retrieving the spears and throwing them down by his son's feet. Lidi watched. Gyre had been hurt in his arm and had not been able to throw spears. Now his father was helping him to learn again. Gyre was going to be a hunter. He was, Lidi knew, only a boy really, but he was going to be a hunter. Her father had said so. Her father had been hurt, too, when they had first come here. He had lain on his bed of skins for many days, and her mother had fed him. Now he was better and would be hunting today. She could hear him inside the hut, re-fastening a loose flint-point with thongs and resin. She hoped he would kill a bear, so that they might have another thick skin on their hut.

Lidi tore the last shred of meat from the smooth bone with her fierce teeth; threw the bone into the fire and watched as it sizzled, turning black. After a while it went white, and crumbled when the embers settled.

'Lidi,' her mother said, 'go down to the trees and gather some bark for kindling. Mind that you find *dry* bark, and do not go too far into the forest.'

Lidi got to her feet.

'I want my bead,' she said, moving towards the doorway.

Reda smiled.

'Yes; you had better wear your bead,' she said.

Lidi went inside to fetch it. It was a bead of amber, which shone, like a wolf's eye, and there was a tiny winged insect with a striped body, right in the middle of it. Old Gart had found it, somewhere, and had made a hole through it, for a thong to go through. He had given it to Lidi and had told her that it would keep her safe if she wore it wherever she went. Since that day she had never failed to wear it around her neck when she left her mother's side. And nothing had ever befallen her, so Lidi knew that Old Gart had told her the truth.

Wrapped in her fox fur, with the bead flashing at her throat, Lidi walked down the slope, the hard ground cold to her bare feet. When she saw that she would have to pass close to where Gyre was throwing his spears she covered the bead with her hands and tried to walk turned away a little. Gyre always teased her about the bead, because he did not believe in it, and called Gart a silly old fool. But Gyre knew what she was covering with her hand and called out: 'Going in the forest, Lidi? Take care, for I saw a bear just nearby today. You need not worry though: you can hit him with your magic bead. Old Gart could have killed all the bears in the forest with that bead.'

Lidi flushed and hurried on. Gyre laughed and she could hear Gawl saying to him, 'I am glad that *you* do not believe Old Gart's tales . . .'

Well; let them laugh. Nothing bad ever happened to her when she wore her bead.

It was darker under the trees, but not so cold as it was up the slope. Lidi was walking on a thick carpet of leaves and if she dug her toes under the top layer, it was quite warm underneath. Old Gart said that some creatures sleep under the leaves all through the winter. Lidi wished that people did, too. Gyre said it was untrue: but where *did* the creatures go in winter, then? She worked steadily down the slope, standing on tiptoe to peel strips of bark from the birches. Soon she had an armful of the kindling, and was about to turn back up the slope, when something attracted her attention. Something white, which moved. There, under a dwarf birch, was a stoat, dressed in its winter coat of ermine. Milky-white, with a black tip on its tail. Lidi moved slowly, setting down her pile of kindling on the ground and looking round cautiously for a stick. An ermine fur was a prize much valued among the people. A stick, or a stone: *something* to throw. Lidi had never hunted anything before, except birds' eggs in the spring, and berries in the autumn. Groping under the leaf mould, her hand found a thick short stick. She raised it slowly behind her head. The stoat sat up, regarding her curiously. Lidi held her breath. Now! The chubby arm swung in a clumsy arc, the stick flew wide, and Lidi sat down heavily on the leaves. The stoat flashed sinuously away and paused atop a fallen tree some distance away, looking back at his fallen adversary. Lidi picked herself up, rearranging her robe and brushing dead leaves from her legs. She pretended not to look at the stoat, over there on its log. Let it go. She didn't care. She sidled closer. Under the roots of the fallen tree was a hole of raw earth with stones in it. She made tiny steps towards it, looking somewhere else, and humming to herself. The stoat could no longer see her. It gazed towards the root, its nose twitching. Lidi knew that the stoat could not see her now. She bent down, and selected some stones of a convenient size, without hurrying. Then she stood up and peered on tiptoe between the curly stiff roots. The stoat was still there. It was licking its forepaws and cleaning its face with them. Lidi crept out from behind the rootclump, doubled. Stones cradled in her left arm, one in her right hand. A pang. She wished Mow were here, with his fish-spear. The stoat stopped washing to gaze at her. Her right arm went up, slowly. The animal shuffled away a little, uneasy, up the trunk. Lidi tensed, and let fly. The stone struck the trunk where the stoat had sat, but it was no longer there. She ran to the tree, reloading her right hand and peered over. The stoat was on the ground beyond, snaking unhurriedly away between the trees. She threw again, missing badly. She could not get over the trunk and when she had run around the root end the stoat was gone. She blew out a sibilant plume of exasperation, dropped her armful of stones, and leaned against the fallen trunk.

Mow would have hit the stoat. She knew he would. She had seen him bring down a waterbird with a well-aimed stone. The bird had waded too close to the pair, as, motionless, they had stood in the reedy shallows, hoping for fish to spear. How proudly they had borne their victim into the village! It had been placed with the rest of the day's catch, to be divided among the people, and Lidi had sensed Mow's pride, and had shared it. She saw in her mind that thin brown figure, strutting across the platform, spear over one shoulder, limp bird on the other, and a wave of loneliness swept over her, for him and for the platform. How she missed it all; she moped all day around the new village; hanging close to her mother, hoping for a small task, or a few words. How quiet everybody was now, except Gyre with his loud laugh, and his boasting. And it was so cold there on the high cliff. She looked down at her feet and shuffled them deep into the leaves. The amber bead swung and spun on its thong. How she missed Old Gart and his wonderful stories.

Away through the trees, something crashed heavily in the crisp bracken. Lidi gazed that way, but could see only the close-packed birches and gloomy twilight between. She looked upwards, through the lattice of delicate tree limbs. The sky had become heavy grey.

A vague unease stirred in her and she moved, trotting back around the groping root end, seeking her pile of bark. Where had she put it down? It must have been just there, where she had pulled the stick from the leaf mould. It was not here. Then where? Panic rose, briefly. Lost in the forest. But no. If she kept on up the slope, she *must* come to the cliff. But she had no kindling. Quickly, she began to work the nearest tree, tearing off strips of bark with scrabbling nails, then moving to one higher up. Something was treading bracken again, nearby. The little girl tore at the trunk, clumsy with fright. A voice inside said, 'Leave the bark! Get up the slope. Run home.'

A crackling tread, and snuffling, quite close. She let the few pathetic flakes fall, peering into the gloom. There. Something moving between the silvery trunks. Something huge and snuffling, coming out of the bracken. Lidi, sobbing in her throat, ran. The noise behind sounded closer. The short, shaky legs worked desperately, pounding the small feet into the leaves. How close it sounded now! Tears of terror dimmed her eyes, and she swung across the slope, then, blindly down! Panic blotted out all thought of direction; only the speed mattered now. Arms flying wildly, the terrified infant ran howling through the trees, and in her whirling mind it seemed that with every flying pace the horror behind her drew nearer. Until somewhere deep in that dim, labyrinthine forest, one small foot hooked a hidden looping root, and Lidi crashed exhausted to the ground. Leaves scattered, then settled around her. Gradually the choking sobs subsided and the small body ceased to heave. Lidi's consciousness flickered out and the first thin flakes of snow sifted down through brooding forest silence.

The pale sun vanished behind clouds that piled up over the forests, rolled forward, and spread out over the lake. Reda, pounding roots by her doorway, became uneasy. Lidi had been gone too long. At length, the woman rose and went down the slope. She was not too worried as yet because she knew that there were many things which might have caught Lidi's interest causing her to forget time. In the fringe of the trees, she stopped, listening. Subdued birdsong, somewhere. The thin wind in the tops. Otherwise, nothing. She called, and the name reverberated down the dim aisles.

'Lidi!'

She listened again. Nothing. The bird had stopped. The wind gusted faintly and somewhere far away . . . something. A long, high echo, like a distant owl scream, or a she-fox under the moon; like some frightened creature, and yet – like no creature Reda had ever heard. Fear seized her abruptly, so that her hand went to her mouth, and she whirled, stumbling uphill and calling with a cracked voice.

'Hila! Jodi!' And again, 'Jodi!'

As she came up to the settlement, the two women ran to meet her, Jodi bouncing Pab over her shoulder. Reda babbled, incoherently.

'Lidi . . . in the forest. Screams. I heard screams . . .'

Hila gripped her by the shoulders, calm.

'How long is she gone?' she asked, crisply.

'Sunrise,' choked Reda. 'Since sunrise, to gather bark . . .'

Jodi glanced at the sky.

'She is not gone long, and cannot be far away. Wait!' She ran with Pab to Hila's hut, where Ela was emerging to discover the cause of the commotion.

'Here! Take Pab. We go to seek Lidi. Make the smoke fire to bring the men!'

And the startled girl, clutching the baby, watched as the three women ran downhill into the trees. Lidi! Lost in the forest! And the men away. Smoke! Call back the men!

Setting Pab down on skins by the doorway, Ela ran towards the fire which burned always in its place between the huts. As she ran, she snatched up handfuls of grass, tearing it out by its roots. She flung two fistfuls of the damp stuff into the glow, and heavy white smoke curled upwards. Then she was off around the settlement, ripping up greenery wherever it grew; nettles, grasses, shrubs; often with soily roots intact. Soon, the sizzling fire emitted a steady column of white which rose straight up for a way, then slanted out over the lake. Finally, Ela snatched a water-skin, poured the contents over a bearskin, and spread this over the smouldering heap. The smoke ascended thickly, as snow began to fall on the deserted settlement. The girl returned to Pab and sat nursing him in the doorway, watching the smoke and the spinning snowflakes and listening to the profound silence.

'I wish that Morg were here,' she thought.

* * *

Morg rubbed the sliver of bone vigorously across the rough stone. The point was coming, slowly. He shuffled a little closer to the fire. A snowflake prickled on his hand, melting. A powdery flurry whirled over the worn boughs of the platform.

'A cold day, to sit making points,' he thought, bitterly. 'A good day to be hunting.'

His father was away with Modd, seeking game. He would have been with them, except for the fact that there were now only two flint-tipped spears left, and no arrowheads. The bone made a rhythmic sound on the stone.

'Bone spear-tips! All right for fishes, or perhaps hares.'

But the fishes stayed deep now, away from the ice-skimmed shallows, and the village could not be fed on the thin hares of winter. He had left his last flint in the shoulder of an elk yesterday – an old bull, which Modd had driven towards him, until he had risen beside it from the scrub and lunged with the spear, as it plunged past in panic. The head had found no vital spot, and had snapped off. The crazed beast had crashed away into the trees, taking with it the precious point, and Daf's last arrow also. Though the three weary men had followed its track for hours thereafter, the beast had not fallen and they had returned meatless to the village. Morg looked across to where his mother squatted, beating roots with a smooth stone. Cyl and Mow had gathered the roots, hacking them from the flint-hard ground with antler picks. There were not many roots, and the people were hungry. In the chief's hut the two ancients sat in grave discussion. Game was scarce, and without the proper weapons, killing was becoming difficult. If the men returned empty-handed tonight, then they must launch an attack tomorrow on the flint beds, despite the dreadful risks.

Morg's belly ached with emptiness. Even the bones had been gathered up and pounded for the marrow inside. No scrap of food remained on the platform, except those roots in his mother's pot. Tonight, if the men brought no meat, the people would share the pulped roots. A handful each of hot mush, perhaps, and another cold, aching night. Perhaps Gawl had been right: perhaps they could not survive the winter. How were the outcasts faring, he wondered? Ela. He wondered particularly about Ela. He lifted his eyes and looked out across the lake. The distant cliff was not visible today, but a column of white smoke stood high over the horizon. Too thick for a cooking-fire. Deliberate smoke: a signal! Morg dropped his bone, and rose to his feet, peering out across the grey distance. The column stood thick and steady; the signal which had always been used by the people, to call back the men to the village, in case of emergency. Morg ran to the chief's hut, crouching in the doorway. The two old men looked up as his shadow darkened the interior.

'Smoke!' he cried. 'A signal, coming from the cliff.'

The chief looked concerned.

'Show us,' he said, crawling through the low doorway, and standing up stiffly.

Old Gart followed him out. Morg pointed. The snow was falling more thickly now, but the smoke was still clearly visible.

'There is trouble over there, certainly,' said the chief, 'and the men will be away. But we are far from the cliff here, and I cannot see how we can help them.'

'Why should we help them? They are causing us to starve!' – this from Mow's mother, who had come over to see what was happening.

Old Gart turned a reproachful look on the angry woman.

'There are women over there; women who were your friends. They are not responsible for what Gawl is doing to us. And there is Lidi; would you have anything happen to Lidi?'

Morg broke in, agitated.

'Let us not waste time in argument!' He turned to the chief. 'Let me go to them. I will run swiftly, taking the game-trail round the north end of the lake. I will be with them by midday.' The old chief pondered a moment.

'The snow falls heavily, Morg,' he said, thoughtfully. 'We do not know the nature of the danger you will find, and we have no good weapon for you to take.'

Morg was determined.

'I have a spear with a bone tip,' he said. 'And my axe. Let me be gone, quickly.'

'Go then; but take great care, for your people here have need of you,' said the chief.

Morg ran over to his father's hut, to get his spear. His mother stood by the doorway.

'Be wary, Morg,' she warned. 'Remember, they are our enemies now, and may not want our help.'

Morg hugged her briefly.

'I shall be safe, Mother. Our common enemies will make us friends again.'

And he was gone, loping off into the snow. His mother stood for a while, watching his dwindling figure. She was afraid for her son, but there was pride in her breast, also.

'You are young, Morg,' she said softly. 'But there is wisdom in what you say.'

He melted into the forest, and the woman sighed, and turned away.

The elk was cornered. Trapped. Behind, the sheer face of a towering crag, overhanging and impassable. Before, this grim, shuffling semicircle of men, advancing relentlessly behind rigid spears. Four men. The elk rolled his eyes for their scent struck terror into him. He backed, until he felt the cold stone at his rump and could back no more. In desperation, he lowered his antlered head and lunged. Gawl jinked sideways, and an ivory point narrowly missed his side. He laughed.

'Take care, Gawl!' cried Alpa. 'He will spear you!'

Gawl prodded at the beast with his spear, goading it. He laughed again, excited.

'No beast alive can spear Gawl,' he panted. 'But I like an animal that fights.'

The elk lunged again, and Gawl leapt back, cat-like. The antlers slashed in an upwards arc, shaving the man's glistening chest.

Gyre, teeth bared, saw the admiration in the eyes of his father's comrades, and he glowed with pride. Gawl was indeed a mighty hunter. Gawl was a fitting leader of men. While their enemies went hungry, Gawl filled the bellies of his people with meat. The discomforts of an ill-chosen camp were forgotten. Here was meat. Here was sport. Here was excitement. The boy grinned, and advanced another step, his spear jabbing at the heaving flank of the elk. Gawl was moving in to challenge his victim again when Trond called, urgently, 'Gawl! Look! The signal!'

A column of smoke above the forest to westward.

'Come!' This from Alpa.

'There is danger. Let us go quickly!'

Gyre lowered his spear. Trond and Alpa, eyes on the west, stepped back. The deadly semicircle broke. The elk saw, and plunged forward.

'Wait!'

A cry, almost a shriek, from Gawl.

'Keep your places. Hold the circle!' The two men looked aghast at their leader, but the half-circle formed again. The spears came up, and the elk backed off, snorting and tossing its head.

'We will take the elk first,' cried Gawl.

'Kill him, then!' shouted Alpa. 'And let us be gone. Our women are in danger.'

Gawl laughed, unpleasantly. Trond took one eye off the beast to glance at him.

'Alpa is right. The signal means come at once. We should leave this,' he said.

Gawl did not even hear. Eyes gleaming with excitement, he was moving in, his spear tip weaving, questing for a vital thrust. Gyre held his position in the tight circle. His spear was pointed at the doomed beast, but his eyes were on his father. The boy had never seen him like this before. It was as though everything in the world had ceased to exist for Gawl, except the snorting, plunging animal before him. He was proud of his brave father, but in that moment a part of Gyre saw the irresponsibility that lay beneath the reckless exterior. Gawl moved in, prodding at the throat of his victim, so that the frantic beast reared, slashing the air with its sharp fore-hooves. Like a flash, Gawl was in underneath those deadly hooves, and his spear took the creature in the soft belly. Then he flung himself aside as the elk came down, squealing and threshing, among the loose boulders. It lay on its side, kicking and gasping, trying to rise. Alpa and Trond moved in. Simultaneous, powerful thrusts and the great beast rolled over, its antlers clashing on the rocks, and lay still. Gawl stood looking down at it for a moment; then motioning to his companions with his bloodied spear, said, 'Now come: we will answer the signal.'

Alpa looked at his leader with surprise.

'Are we to leave the elk here, to be eaten by wolves?' he cried.

Gawl turned on him, angrily.

'There is danger. Would you linger to cut up a dead elk while our people die?'

Gawl's excitement had died with the elk, and he acted now as though his own recent refusal to answer the signal had never happened. Trond thrust his spear into the snow-flecked grass, to clean off some of the blood.

'We lingered to kill it,' he muttered.

Gawl snorted.

'You chose me for your leader. You do not grumble when I fill your bellies with meat. You dance and sing when I defeat our enemies at the flint-digging. Come, let us be gone, and do not presume to question my leadership.'

The three hunters and the boy, pulling their robes about them against the snow, shouldered their weapons and turned towards the smoke signal, moving at a steady lope. Nothing more was said, but Gyre did not fail to notice the questioning glances which passed between Alpa and Trond, as they wove their course between the trees, following their strange leader.

Morg slowed to a walk at the foot of the slope and moved cautiously through the last trees, peering through the whirling snow towards the settlement on the open rise ahead. Nothing stirred. Three tents, white-capped now, and still. Nearby, a smoking fire. No sound. The boy held his spear ready and stepped into the open, walking quickly uphill. Between the huts, he stopped, listening. An abrupt sound. He spun round, facing the hut from whence the sound came. In the doorway Ela crouched, gazing at him.

'Morg!' she cried. 'Why do you come here? There is danger for you.'

'I saw the signal,' he replied. 'What is wrong?'

Ela emerged, straightening up.

'Lidi. She is lost in the forest. The women are gone to search for her. The men have not returned yet. Perhaps they do not see the smoke.'

Morg looked down towards the trees.

'They will come,' he told her. 'The smoke can be seen a great distance.' He looked at the girl. 'How is it with you?' he enquired softly.

She shrugged, her face sad.

'It is well. We are cold, but there is meat. I miss our people.'

Morg nodded.

'It is different now you are gone, also,' he said. 'We are cold, too.' He stepped back. 'I will seek Lidi. If I find her, I will bring her here.'

Ela looked at him, afraid.

'Take care, Morg,' she warned. 'Gawl and Gyre hate you. They would kill you, even while you helped them.'

Morg nodded.

'When they come, tell them I am searching too. Tell them that it would be better if I might use *both* my eyes to seek Lidi, rather than keeping one eye open for them!'

He turned and walked rapidly downhill. In the fringe of the trees he looked back. She was standing there, dim in the snow. She saw him pause and raised her arm. He waved in reply and walked into the forest. A short way down, Morg heard people approaching. He flattened himself against a tree, waiting. Reda was crying softly and Hila was trying to comfort her. When they came level, he stepped out in front of them. The women stopped, startled. Silencing their exclamation, he questioned them, rapidly. They had found nothing, except a bundle of bark-strips on the ground. They had walked through the trees, calling the child's name, until they could go no further for cold and exhaustion and had made their way back. Morg glanced at the heavy sky. It would be daylight for some time yet. Urging the bedraggled women to await their men at the settlement and offering some words of comfort to Reda he strode on, intent upon covering as much ground as possible before dark.

No sooner had the women's voices faded behind him, however, than Morg heard others somewhere ahead of him. Again he concealed himself, and presently four figures came into view. Morg recognised Gawl and his fellow conspirators. Alpa was walking lamely, holding his side, and the others were urging him on. Morg emerged, walking towards them with his spear over his shoulder as a sign of his peaceful intentions. Gyre saw him first and called a shrill warning to the others, advancing his own spear to cover the others. The four stopped, warily. Trond and Gawl raised their spears, also, but Alpa used his to support himself, gasping and clutching his side with his free hand. There was blood on his wolfskin.

'Put up your spears,' said Morg, stopping before them. 'I am here in answer to the signal.'

Gawl growled: 'The signal is for us, from our people, and does not concern you.'

'Lidi's fate concerns us all,' flashed back Morg.

Alpa stared. 'Lidi!' he cried. 'What has happened to Lidi?'

Morg turned to the injured man.

'Your daughter is lost somewhere out here,' he said. 'Tell these fools to put up their spears. I am here to help.'

Alpa appealed to Gawl.

'Let our quarrel rest, Gawl,' he pleaded. 'It will be dark soon, and it is cold. We must find her quickly.'

Gawl gazed at the boy before him. He hated Morg

with a bitter hatred. But his followers would not forgive him if he put his own feelings before the safety of the child.

'Very well,' he agreed, sullenly. 'We will go different ways. Alpa, you cannot help with your wound open again. Go to the camp and tell the women we are searching.'

He turned to Trond and Gyre.

'Go as far as you can, but leave yourselves enough time to return to camp by dark. Anyone caught by darkness in the forest is dead.'

To Morg he said, 'If *you* find her, as darkness overtakes you, you may take refuge with us tonight. Tomorrow you will go and never approach our settlement again.'

Alpa, fearful for his little girl, was reluctant to return to camp, but the spear-wound in his side had been opened by his running, and he knew he could not continue. He looked at his companions, pleadingly.

'Find her,' he said in a choked voice. 'If she is still unfound when night comes, then she will go to the lost ones.' Then he turned and stumbled off, towards the camp. Gawl pointed to the north.

'Gyre and Trond. You go that way. I will go there; and you,' he pointed south, looking at Morg, 'you go that way. We will meet at dark, at the camp.'

The four parted, moving softly on the powdery snow that now covered the forest floor. Once Morg looked back, to find that Gyre had stopped and was watching him through the white silence. The two regarded each other for a moment and then turned and walked on. Morg hunched his shoulders to bury his stinging ears in the fur of his robe. He was hungry. Somewhere out there, he thought, is Lidi. A picture came to his mind of the child, as she had been in the yellow warmth of the summer: humming like a bee to herself as she bustled absorbed, brown and naked, about her mysterious business up and down the sunlit slopes. And he dismissed the cold and the hunger and thoughts of friends who now were enemies, and plunged on into the silver solitude.

Her body felt warm, but her hands and feet were icy. She was lying cocooned in something soft and feathery, like a dream of ermine from which she was slowly waking. Something cold ran across her chest and seeped into the corner of her mouth. She opened her eyes. White, everywhere. Memory stirred, and the warm white dream melted away. Snow. She was lying in snow. It had been snowing, and she had fallen. Running. Running from . . . the bear! A whimper of fear, and Lidi moved, trying to rise. Snow scattered from her shoulders as she sat up, stiffly, and looked quickly all around. Nothing. A soft white carpet of white, and silvery naked trees with their heads in the heavy sky. And the flakes drifting down in silence. She wanted to go back into her dream. It was warm there. Everything was ermine. Her feet did not ache there nor were her fingers blue and stiff. Her hair did not hang wet over her shoulders and there was no dull ache of hunger in her belly. She would go back.

Lidi's head drooped and she lowered herself gently towards the snow blanket. The amber bead spun and glowed beneath her heavy eyes. Old Gart. They were close to the fire. So close to the delicious crackling fire, and her face burned and her back was cold and Old Gart was telling a story . . . 'but the great beast never fell, and his track led on and on through the snow; and Tota followed, growing colder and colder and more and more tired, until he fell down in the snow. And the snow became a bed of fur for Tota, and the cold stone of his hunger melted in his belly, and he dreamed a warm dream, until the lost ones came and carried him away . . .'

Lidi shook her head, vigorously, to disperse the shreds of her dream. No. She must not dream. It was the warm dream of Tota, and the lost ones wait for those who dream it. She sat up, chafing her feet with aching hands, until the feet ached also. She blew on her fingers, grimacing with the pain. She looked at the sky. It was darkening, and she was lost. The snowflakes blew into her face, tingling, and mingled with the warm tears there. Lidi pulled her garment a little closer around her body, shivering, and stood up. Snow fell from the robe, as she walked slowly between the trees. Her frightened, weary mind made a picture for her of her mother, who seemed to stand before her, arms outstretched, saying 'Come' with her gentle eyes; but moving backwards, elusively, as Lidi moved forward. So that the tiny figure held out its fat brown arms to emptiness and murmured 'Mama' as it stumbled along. And a trail of prints, winding away back through the muffled aisles marked the way that Lidi came.

Morg picked up the tracks as the light was fading. He had been about to turn back along his own tracks, sick at heart, when he spotted the place where the child had lain; a scuffed hollow with her small footprints all around, where she had stamped the life back into her feet. The boy saw where the aimless double row meandered away under the birches. The pathetic trail called him to follow; but the creeping gloom repelled him with a fear that came from deep within; a fear of the night implanted through countless generations of his forebears. The spear in his hand, puny even in the daylit woods, held no hope of protection in the phantom-ridden forests of the night. If he followed the child, they would meet, probably, only in the land of the lost ones, from which there is no going back. Somewhere, a long way off, a wolf howled, and Morg shuddered. But a wolf at least is real and can be seen in daylight. Morg's fear was of those other presences, which Old Gart spoke of; creatures of no known form or substance, which were never seen; only *felt* in the heart. Morg had no doubt that they existed for he could feel them now. He ought to turn, and run through the dwindling twilight to the sanctuary of the firelight. To the fire of his enemies, who were only men, and could be met on equal terms. No man can fight the lost ones. No spear can wound the things that come in the night; to try, vainly, to assuage their abysmal hunger with the hearts of the doomed.

Lidi. Such a tiny heart. Such a small voice to call for ever out of the darkness beyond the firelight. And Reda, who would turn her head from the fire in the night, and hope, with an aching hope, to see that which no man ever sees; whose heart would go each night where her feet dare never follow.

And Morg, the half-man, gripped his weapon and, clenching his teeth, walked where the child's tracks led. The sun, behind its shroud of grey, dipped below the western forest, and darkness flooded the land. Only the steady mush of the boy's feet in the snow broke the silence. Morg strained to hear. They were all around him now. Once he threw up his spear, knowing it would be futile; and an owl ghosted by on velvet wings.

The tracks stretched away through the haunted trees until skeletal birch gave way to dense pine, and Morg could track no more. For here, the snow lay heavy upon the pine boughs above and none lay on the fragrant needle-carpet. And though the cloud broke and a sickle moon glowed fitfully in the frigid sky, nothing existed to mark the passage of the child. Morg walked on a little among the laden pines. The shadows of their trunks latticed the crackling floor, and sometimes a tiny avalanche of snow fell from a bough with a soft thud. After a time, the boy stopped. The silence was absolute. Nothing stirred. As far as his eyes could penetrate, in every direction, lay the carpet of pine-needles. If he walked further, he would become lost himself. If he turned back, there was his own trail, where formless, nameless things lurked to cut off his retreat. Deep within himself, Morg knew that the lost ones must have taken the child already. If he came back tomorrow with the men from her village he knew that they would find nothing. It had always been so. The night does not give up its victims. Sadly, he turned, and began to retrace his steps. His breath hung in plumes of white on the frosty air. The sense of being watched by unseen eyes was overpowering so that, as he walked, he turned his head, first one way, then the other, knowing all the time that he would never see the thing that waited for him, that would come with a silent, awful glide from the blackness, to envelop him in ghastly folds of everlasting night.

With the tail of his eye, he saw it. Back among the pines. A single, unwinking eye, baleful under the moon. The thing crouched behind a scrub-pine, watching him with its one eye. No owl, this. A formless darkness, close to the ground behind that stunted pine. He stopped. His spear pointed towards the thing, and the hands that held it trembled: a puny ivory point, to defy the unimaginable forces of darkness. He screwed his eyes and imagined he saw it move forward, one quick pace and flatten again. A glance behind. Out there, others would be moving in on him also. All around, liquid shadows, stalking the night. He was finished. He knew it with a cold and heavy certainty. But Morg was a proud boy, descended of a proud line, and he would meet his end as his fathers had met theirs: fighting to the last and spitting defiance in the face of that which overwhelmed him.

Eyes fixed upon that terrible single eye he ran, bounding over the moonlit snow, spear high, the hunting-cry of his fathers on his lips. The thing seemed to bunch itself to meet his charge and Morg's arm went back for his last, hopeless throw. The things of the night would win; but they would know that they had fought with a warrior.

In the instant of throwing, he checked. His point of aim had been the glowing eye, and, close now to the stunted tree through which it glared, he saw that the eye hung by a thread among the dark needles and spun very slowly, first one way and then the other. And the moonlight caught its uneven surfaces, so that it flashed a little as it turned. Beyond the dwarf pine was a long shallow depression in the ground; the shadowy thing which he had defied with the courage of ignorance. And at the bottom of that depression, far gone in the warm dream of Tota: Lidi. The boy flung down his weapon and with a sob of thankfulness, knelt beside the tiny girl, gathering her up, and holding her small, cold form tightly to his thick robe. How long he remained like that, rocking the little creature slowly from side to side he never knew. But presently she stirred; the first fluttering of returning life; and soon, senseless still, but knowing somehow that she was saved, she clung sleeping to the warm wolfskin as he rose, stiffly, and retrieved his spear. Pausing to pluck the amber bead from the tree, and to rehang it gently round Lidi's neck, Morg moved off. One arm held the infant and the spear was defiant in the crook of the other.

Slowly, and in constant dread, he trekked back along his own faint trail. The unseen watchers lurked at every hand. But the bead bobbed and spun and glowed; and the shadows fell back before him, and he passed between them, unscathed.

It was close to dawn when Trond, tending the low fire at the cliff camp, saw the shadowy form approaching, up the slope. He reached for his spear, and backed away as the figure came into the fire glow, revealing itself as Morg, with a small burden. Trond's voice came hoarse with fright.

'Lost ones cannot approach the fire,' he whispered.

Morg laid his burden gently by the embers, and smiled wearily.

'We are not lost, Trond,' he replied. 'You can put up your spear, for we are men like you.'

And Trond came close, and touched the boy on the shoulder, before he would believe. And he said, 'No man has ever walked the forest in the night, and returned to tell of it. Why did the lost ones not take you, Morg, and the child?'

Morg shrugged.

'I do not know, Trond,' he said. 'I will never know.'

But Lidi knew. When the joyful reunion was over: when the light washed away the last of the fear, so that the thing between Morg and the other men returned, and he slipped away down the crisp hill into the morning forest; lying among soft furs in Reda's lodge, Lidi knew. And she slept, with the amber bead clutched tightly in one tiny hand.

6

The cliff settlement lay quiet under the grey morning sky. Smoke from the fire started up and outward across the lake. On one side of the fire, huddled together, sat Gawl, Trond and Alpa, their garments of thick fur pulled closely around their shoulders. Gawl had admitted at last that his camp site would be constantly swept by the east wind, and so had built a windbreak of supple boughs, woven together, on the eastern side of the fire. The three men sat with their backs to this. Against the other side of the windbreak, a snowdrift had built up, and now, not even the keenest wind could find a way through. Nobody else could be seen about the settlement, for the people had been driven to seek the shelter of their huts by the bitter cold. Cooking was done inside now, over earthen bowls of melted fat, in which floated wicks of animal skin which gave a little light, and a little heat. The meat took a long time to cook. It was smoky in the huts but although their eyes smarted, and they choked when they breathed, nobody ventured outside unless it were absolutely necessary, except the three hunters.

Beside the fire an argument was in progress. The insistent voice of Gawl pierced the frigid air.

'He is my son, and I am your leader. I will have him a hunter, and I will listen to no dissension.'

Gawl's face was red with anger, as it always was when anybody dared to disagree with him. Alpa was the object of his anger this time.

Alpa spoke again, quietly, but insistently.

'But he is a boy of few summers, and not yet ready for manhood. If there were others of his age here, they would play together as children, and he with them.' He appealed to Trond, who sat frowning beside him. 'Trond. How say you? Should a boy of Gyre's age hunt with us, and sit in council?'

Trond pondered a moment in silence. He was not thinking about the wisdom of allowing Gyre into the rights of manhood. He was thinking about the foolishness of disagreeing with Gawl. Gawl scowled at him, waiting for his reply. He said, 'Perhaps Gawl is right. We are only three, and game is scarce. Four would hunt better than three.'

Gawl grunted his approval. Alpa spoke again to Trond. 'But the boy hunts with us already. He need not be admitted to manhood in order to do that.'

Trond only grunted, and looked away.

'He is the son of a chief,' cried Gawl imperiously, 'and I will have him a man!'

The courageous Alpa tried again. 'Boys become men,' he said softly, 'as they grow in body and in skill; not when commanded to do so. Gyre is not grown enough in either to kill his bear.'

Gawl turned on him, furious.

'There will *be* no bear! My son becomes a man because *I* declare him so! If you would continue your opposition to me, Alpa, then do so with your spear!'

Now Alpa spoke angrily.

'If we fight over this matter, then one of us will die, and we shall be but *two* hunters and a child. Besides, matters of council were never settled with spears; neither did boys ever become men without killing their first bear.'

Gawl leapt to his feet, teeth bared.

'This council is conducted according to *my* law, and will decide as *I* decide!'

'Then it is no council!' cried Alpa, rising to face his leader.

'So be it!' roared Gawl. '*I* shall be your council, and my son shall help me in my task!'

Alpa trembled with anger. Even Trond looked horrified.

'You will lead us to our deaths, you and your child!' hissed Alpa.

Gawl spat contemptuously, at the feet of his followers.

'You chose my leadership. If you despise the wisdom that fills your bellies, then return to the platform, and die!'

'You could not hold the flintbed against all of us, Gawl,' Alpa cried, 'even with your puppy prancing at your side.'

'Against *all* of you?' queried Gawl. 'All of you? You fool! There *are* no others. They are dead of hunger and cold. The wolves have had the marrow of their bones by now and the mice lie fattened in their hollow skulls!'

Trond glanced wide-eyed towards the lake.

'It is true, Alpa,' he whispered dryly. 'There has been no smoke for many days now. We are alone.'

Gawl threw up his arms in a gesture of triumph.

'Alone!' he cried. 'And lords of the forest!'

Alpa shuddered.

'Alone, perhaps, in the daytime: and lords of the forest, until the dark. But so small, in the night, in the glow from our fire; and the lost ones, whom we have starved, ringed all about at our backs, waiting in the trees, waiting . . .'

Gawl laughed, loudly.

'Let them wait! They will wait for ever.'

His laughter echoed away through the brittle woods.

'No, Gawl,' breathed Alpa, his eyes sad. 'Not for ever.'

If Gawl heard he did not heed.

'Assemble my people!' he cried. 'It shall be done as I have decreed!'

They came, shivering, from their huts, to squat as close to the fire as they could, huddled in their furs. Gawl stood erect before them, and called his son to stand beside him. Gyre rose and stood beside his father, wondering why he was asked to do so. Gawl put a hand on the boy's thin shoulder.

'Today,' he said, in ringing tones, 'my son becomes a man. Henceforth, he hunts for my people, and sits with me in council!'

A gasp arose from the squatting people. Jodi, holding Pab, said softly: 'No . . . oh no!'

She cast fear-filled eyes upon the thin boy. Her son was too young, too small. She spoke up.

'Gawl. Our son is not yet grown enough to face his bear alone. Do not send him from whence he will never return.' Her voice was desperate. Gawl turned on her.

'It is not for a woman to question the decision of the council,' he rapped.

'It was no council!' cried Alpa.

Gawl whirled to face him.

'Silence! Or you will feel the keenness of my spear!'

Reda cried, 'Let *all* the people decide!'

Gawl spun to face the woman. There was fear in his eyes now, behind the anger.

'*I* have decided!' he hissed. 'What *I* say will be done.'

There was now a general hubbub; everybody talking and arguing with everybody else. Gyre stood bewildered. A mixture of emotions swirled within him. How wonderful to be a man: to be a hunter, while Morg, if he still lived, was but a boy! But the idea of facing a bear alone; he, who had killed only hares and frogs and fishes! He shuddered, and turned a little pale. And to become a man in the face of all this opposition by the people . . . He looked at his father, appealingly.

'Father . . . I do not know if . . .'

'Silence!' roared Gawl. 'You will do as I say!' He faced the people, raising his voice above theirs. 'There will be no bear! I have decreed that my son is a man, and that is sufficient. From this day, let him be accorded the respect due to a man and to a hunter.'

Gyre breathed his relief, silently. No bear! Manhood, respect, and no price to pay. The people became silent. Every eye was upon Gawl. Jodi sat back, content. For her, the respect due to the mother of a hunter. She smiled faintly, and looked upon her slight son with eyes no longer fearful, and then upon Gawl, with pride. Ela, beside her mother, gazed at the now jubilant youth. She knew of his hatred for Morg: and though she knew that the hatred was not returned by the older boy, she herself disliked Gyre intensely. He had always been a braggart, a bully and, she suspected, something of a coward. Always he had vented his aggressions upon those weaker than himself; upon small children and small creatures. And always he had basked in the reflected glory of his headstrong and dashing father. Now, he was to be a man, while Morg remained a boy. The injustice of it stung her, and the thought that Morg might no longer be even a boy, brought tears to her eyes. How Gyre would crow! How he would strut. Her brimming eyes burned at him, and she moved her lips in quiet contempt.

'Your first bear would be your last,' she breathed.

Gyre, holding himself proudly, did not see. The great spear was brought, and placed in his hands. Its haft was almost as thick as the boy's arm. He swore, as Morg had sworn, to use it well for the people. The people! He looked down into their intent, upturned faces. Alpa: burningly hostile. Reda: a blank face; perhaps a faint twist at the corner of her mouth. Trond: carefully blank, eyes upon Gawl. Hila: lips compressed, hostile. His mother: returning his haughty stare with one of complacent pride. Lidi: looking nowhere in particular, and clicking that ridiculous bead on her teeth. Ela.

The boy's eyes rested upon Ela. Eyes of liquid fire. Crying? The mixture of hatred and sorrow baffled him. A pretty girl, whom the women said would be a beautiful woman. Morg's woman. Gyre's eyes flashed with sudden malice, and he leaned and spoke softly to his father. The watching people saw a slow grin spread over Gawl's face, and he held up his hand for attention.

'My people!' he began. 'There is among us, one who was promised to the son of a chief. But he, who once walked through the night with the lost ones, now walks thus for ever.'

Ela caught her breath sharply, and gazed up at the swaggering Gawl as though hypnotised. Something, she knew, was about to happen regarding herself: something terrible. Gawl continued.

'Ela was promised to the son of a chief. Now there is only *one* chief, and *Gyre* is his son.' Father and son gazed down at the stricken girl. 'In the spring,' went on Gawl, 'before we journey into the hills, my son will claim Ela for his woman.'

Ela's head spun. She saw the hated youth grinning down at her in malicious triumph. She covered her face with her hands, sobbing violently.

'No! No! No!' she choked.

Her mother pulled the shuddering girl close, and glared up at Gawl.

'You cannot do this. Ela is promised to Morg, and we do not know that he is dead!' Tears of desperation were on her cheeks. Gawl only sneered, and Hila turned to her man.

'Trond! This cannot be. Tell him that this cannot be!' Trond looked at Hila, then up at the scowling Gawl, then back again at Hila, and shrugged.

'Why not?' he asked. 'Gyre will be chief one day, and our daughter will be his woman. It will be the same as if she had become Morg's woman.'

Ela tore herself free from her mother, and turned to her father.

'The same?' she shrieked. 'The same?'

She pointed a trembling hand at Gyre.

'That ugly creature will never be even half the man Morg will be!' She leapt to her feet and faced the youth, her hands clenched.

'I will never come to you . . . you . . . frog!' she screamed. 'Morg is *not* dead, and one day, he will make you sorry you ever dared look upon me!'

And then she turned from him, running over the snow to her father's hut, and ducked inside.

Gawl, his face purple with fury, snatched the spear from his son and, brandishing it, screamed, 'Everything shall be as I say! Everything! Everything! Everything!'

Eyes blazing, he slashed around him with the spear, until the circle broke, and the people moved uncertainly away, towards their own huts. Soon, father and son were alone beside the fire.

Towards night, the cloud broke, and the ragged pieces went hurrying westward under the cold moon. Trond huddled close to the fire, feeding it from time to time, and shivering in spite of the crackling warmth. Keeper of the fire was no easy task on a night such as this. Back at the platform, there had been seven men to share the duty, for the chief, and even Old Gart, had taken their turns. Now it was his turn every third night. A lonely task. Long, cold, and lonely. Longer now, because there was no old man to keep the people round the fire far into the night with his tales. Trond glanced around him. No glimmer of light showed in any of the three doorways. All the lamps had gone out: everybody was asleep. He gazed into the blackness of his own doorway. For a long time, there had been the sound of sobbing from within, and the soft crooning of Hila, comforting her distraught daughter. Now it had ceased. Trond shrugged into the darkness. Well, the girl would get used to the idea. And anyway, it was no small thing to be the woman of a future chief. He had, he told himself, done the right thing. He was a good father. And a part of him said no, quietly and insistently, so that he was glad to tear his mind away from the subject, and listen to the distant howling of the wolves.

Ela had stopped crying; but she was not asleep. She breathed slowly and evenly, as though she was sleeping, until her mother stopped stroking her hair, and slept herself. Then she lay a while thinking, and listening to the wolves, and the wind, and a faraway owl. She shivered.

'How can I do it?' she thought. 'How can *anybody* do it?'

And yet Morg had done it. Deep into the forest night, and back again, carrying little Lidi. No man had ever returned before from such a journey. They said it was the bead. The amber bead, guiding his footsteps, and driving back the lost ones from his path. Some said that. Gawl said the lost ones spared him for a worse fate that awaited him. Gyre said that, too, and even went into detail about what that fate might be. Thinking of Gyre made her shudder, and she sat up, quietly. She was more calm now, and quite determined. She moved stealthily, finding in the dark her thickest robe, which was white and would be difficult to see against the snow. Her mother slept on. Ela knelt in a corner of the hut, swiftly lashing tight a small bundle with a thong. She glanced through the doorway. The fire burned low, and her father nodded over it. She felt a pang for him. He was a weak man, and he had so admired Gawl. She was sure that now he must have realised his mistake, but it was too late. Now he was sleeping on watch, and she was about to bring him further trouble, for in the morning Gawl would know that he had done so. She hardened her heart. Her father would have let Gyre claim her, knowing how miserable that would make her. Very well, then let him face his angry leader tomorrow, as he ought to have done today. She looked at the dark place where she knew her mother lay. Her lips quivered, and moved, silently.

'You knew my sadness, and sang to me as to a baby,' she whispered. 'Your fingers in my hair were not stilled, until you thought I slept; only then did you sleep yourself. It was always so, my mother, since the first days of my life. And now I must go, while you sleep. You lose your child, and know it not. You will grieve: for tomorrow, if I am not with the lost ones, you will think me so. You will hear my weeping in the trees.' She stifled a sob. 'And wherever I am, my mother, I will hear yours. I *will* hear yours.'

The spiteful wind stung her tear-wet cheeks when she crawled, silent, through the doorway, and the frosted grasses burned beneath her palms. The bead. She must have the bead. Trond nodded still in the firelight. She must stay beyond the glow. She suppressed a shudder, thought deliberately of Gyre, and crawled noiselessly towards the hut of Alpa.

Ela reached the doorway without rousing her father. The fire cast a faint, flickering light on the hut, and she knew that if he looked in her direction, Trond would see her shadow on the wall. She slipped into the black entrance, holding her breath, and groping cautiously before her with one hand. Heavy breathing told her where Alpa lay, between the door and his family. His spear, she knew, would be ready at his side. One sound, and she would die like an animal. With infinite patience, she worked her way over the skin-covered floor, staying close to the walls. His breathing told her that Alpa was now between her and the door. She crawled on, her shoulder brushing the wall. Once, her questing hand found a stack of earthen bowls, and working her way around them, she touched the stack with one knee. There was a dull click, which sounded loud in the black silence. Alpa grunted, turning in his sleep, and the girl froze. When his breathing was again even, she went on. Her eyes were adjusting now to the darkness in the hut and she could make out objects and people as shadowy forms, more solid than the surrounding gloom. When she discovered where the child was lying, Ela almost gasped with dismay. Hila was lying across one corner of the hut, and in the small triangle of floor between her body and the meeting of two walls, lay Lidi. There was no way of working her way around them. Ela would have to reach across the sleeping woman.

Silent as mist, she raised herself to a kneeling position, and strained her eyes to determine Lidi's position. The child lay curled on her side, knees drawn up almost to her chin. Her face was close to her mother's breast, and Hila's arm was flung across the child's shoulder. And somewhere in that small, warm darkness between the two bodies lay the amber bead. Ela drew her knife from the belt at her waist. She slipped her left hand down between the unconscious pair, feeling for the thong that held the bead. Hila's breath was on the back of her hand, and Lidi's on her palm. The hand trembled, and Ela fought to control it. One slip: Alpa's spear would pierce her back and all would be over. Vaguely, she wondered what they would think she had been about to do. Stab Hila? Lidi? There would be her drawn knife. She dismissed the thought, telling herself angrily to concentrate upon the task before her. At last, when she thought that she must scream out with the unbearable tension, her moist fingers found the thong, curled invisibly in that tiny space of beaten earth. Gently, she hooked one shaking finger beneath it, and with infinite care began to raise it, until she could see its thin blackness curling over her finger and down across the child's sleeping face. Taking painful care to allow the thong to remain slack along its length, she bent forward, clenched her teeth around it, and tautened a short length between her mouth and her left hand. A deft slash with the knife; another; and the thong parted. The bead now lay free, somewhere along its length. She felt along the greasy strip of hide, praying that her fingers would not encounter the big knot with which it had been tied: if the bead were on the *other* side of that knot, then it would have to pass beneath the child's neck to be free. When she felt the smoothness of the bead, Ela had to suppress a sigh of thankfulness. She slid it along the thong, until it lay in her palm. Delicately, she lowered the severed ends of hide back into that frightfully small space between mother and child. Silently, she rehung her knife. Then, with the bead in her mouth for safe keeping, she was gone, wraithlike, around the wall, and out into the night.

By the outside wall, she flattened. Trond was poking at the fire with a stick, and gazing vacantly around him. Sparks whirled away briefly and died of cold. The hunter's face was orange with the glow. Ela was suddenly aware of how cold she was. Her naked feet lay like stones in the hoary grass. She lay still. Presently, her father's head fell forward, and he dozed again. She went swiftly on all fours, out of the firelight, and down the snowy slope. The frost-crust crunched a little beneath her hands and knees; she did not pause, or go more slowly: she was beyond the firelight, and no man would follow her here. The moon showed fitfully, and the first trees were close before her. In their thin cover, she rose to her feet, her back against an ice-lacquered trunk, and looked back. No sound came from the settlement and no movement, save for the slow curling of smoke where her father, invisible beyond the windbreak, tended the fire which was life to the people. She had time now to feel the fear. Never before had she ventured so far from fire in the night. And her journey had only begun. The cold soaked to her marrow, and the fear; so that she shuddered without control. She put her numb hand to her mouth and rolled the warm bead into it. Her faith in that bead to lead her, and her loathing of Gyre behind her: without them, she would have gone no further. But the bead had protected Morg and Morg lay at the end of her journey, whether in this life or the next. With a last backward glance, she turned and walked quickly downhill between the trees.

Ela went swiftly, and her eyes darted fearfully this way and that. The wind gusted in the tops with a slow rhythm, so that the forest seemed to breathe. Far away, the high, thin cries of wolves hung like icicles on the air. The girl sobbed quietly to herself from time to time and her breath made a cloud of faint luminosity around her head. Her footfalls crunched on the thin snow with a regular beat, like the blood that beat in her temples. She was listening to them without knowing that she was. How many footfalls from the cliff to the platform? Was she following Morg's exact path, when he walked away around the northern end of the lake, after his rescue of Lidi? Was he still alive? Or had that 'worse fate' of which Gyre spoke, overtaken him? She allowed the thoughts to chase one another across her mind; anything to avoid dwelling upon the nameless horrors that were all around her now. And something, nevertheless, was impinging. Among all the thoughts, impressions and emotions to which she was allowing free rein, some small, insistent signal was clamouring for her attention. She quickened her pace, and sought, sobbing, to drive it away. But it was still there. Count the footfalls. Thud; thud; thud; one foot and then the other. And something more. She stopped; and the footfalls continued. She whirled. Nothing was visible. The footfalls, light and rapid, had been behind her; were approaching still from that direction. Ela, half mad with terror, flattened against a tree; clutching the bead and gibbering soft wild nonsense at it: straining her eyes back along the tracks. Cloud covered the moon, abruptly, and tree-shadows melted into general gloom. The sounds continued, coming nearer. Soft slap and crunch, rapid; and panting, like an eager wolf. Hopelessly, she drew the knife. There was in Ela a spirit like Morg's spirit, and they would pay dear in taking her.

It was very close now, and going more slowly. Ela saw movement, vague in the dark. A shape, low, indistinct; following her own tracks doggedly. She gripped the knife. Its flint blade gleamed dully.

'When it is within one leap, I will strike,' she resolved, grimly, holding her terror in check.

The thing came closer, panting, and making little whining noises. It was a man's length from her tree, and she crouched, teeth bared, to spring. The cloud veil slipped from the face of the moon, and Ela gasped. There, close enough to touch, in a splash of cold radiance, stood Lidi. The child saw her at the same instant. There was no fear, nor even surprise. Her face lit up, and she ran forward, arms outstretched before her.

'Ooh Ela! I have followed you *so* far, and you go so fast!' she cried.

The fat arms went around Ela's thighs, and the tangled head buried itself in her robe. Ela, weak with relief, could only hold the infant tightly, whispering over and over, 'Lidi! Oh! Lidi . . . !'

After a moment Lidi pulled herself free, stepped back, and looked up at Ela, with a small frown between her eyes.

'Why didn't you ask me for my bead, Ela?' she demanded.

'You . . . *saw* me take it?' gasped Ela. 'And you said nothing; didn't even move!'

Lidi looked grave.

'I didn't *see* you take it; I only *felt* you. But I knew it was you because I heard my father saying to my mother that you should run away, and my mother said, "She should take the bead and go in the night," and I was going to give it to you tomorrow.'

Ela crouched, and gave the infant a hug.

'Thank you, Lidi, for not giving me away.' Her face became grave. 'But now I must take you back; perhaps it was not a very good idea to run away. There has been no smoke from the platform for *so* long. Perhaps they are all dead by now.'

Her voice broke as she spoke the last words.

Lidi pouted stubbornly, shaking her head.

'No! I am running away, too. It is cold there, and I have nobody to play with.'

'No, Lidi. You must go back. Your mother will believe you are gone to the lost ones.'

The child shook her head again, emphatically.

'My mother knows that I have my bead,' she said, evenly. 'Nothing bad can happen to me with my bead, and I want to play hunters and women again with Mow.'

Ela gazed at the earnest child. She felt tears come into her eyes.

'Hunters and women,' she breathed, smiling faintly. 'Yes, Lidi; so do I.'

Lidi's glance was sceptical.

'But *you* are grown up!' she said. Ela nodded, and her eyes had a far-away look.

'Yes. Yes, Lidi; I think that I am,' she said. 'Come: we must leave a sign, so that our people will know we met here, and went on together. Help me pull some long grasses in bunches. Like this.' Ela pulled a fistful of long, dead stalks from a clump, and bent the bunch double. Then she wound more stalks tightly around it at the part farthest away from the ends, so that she had something that looked roughly like a doll, with the bound part for a neck, the loop above the binding for a head, and the long ends for body and legs. This she stuck upright in the snow, beside their footprints. Old Gart had made such things for Lidi. 'We've made a doll,' she said.

'This one is me,' Ela told her. Deftly, she made a much smaller doll, and stood it beside the first. 'This one is you,' she said. Lastly, she took a twig, snapped it in the middle, and laid it before the two dolls, with its fracture pointing towards the distant platform. 'Now they will know we were together and where we are going,' she said, straightening up. 'Come: your feet are cold. I will carry you a while.'

So they moved on; Ela going slowly, with the exhausted child sleeping soon in her arms. And the two dolls stood in the snow, and gazed mutely down the new trail that wound bravely through the haunted night.

Blackness paled to pearl between the birch tops, and the gloom withdrew, shrinking quietly away. Silent silver boles, revealed anew, stood stiffly with their frigid feet in snow.

Ela squeezed the little hand in hers, and nodded at the sky.

'See, Lidi; the night is going. The lost ones cannot hurt us any more.'

There was a raw, hot feeling in her eyelids, and a muzzy weight behind in her head. Lidi lifted her puffy face, where tears of fear and weariness had left their mark, and clawed back tangled hair with her free hand.

'I'm cold,' she mumbled, 'and I want to go to sleep.'

Ela squeezed a tight smile for the child. 'Soon, we shall be at the raft,' she said, 'and we can eat, and be warm.'

The little girl shook her head, sullen. 'No! Gawl says there is *no* food at the raft, and no fire. I want to go back.'

Ela grunted, angrily.

'Go back! We are *never* going back. Better we die in the forest.'

She moved doggedly, slurring her numb feet. The infant dragged a little.

'Can't walk any more.' The small moist hand jerked from its warm place, and Lidi sat down in the snow. The older girl stopped, turning uneasily to regard the child.

'Come on, Lidi.' There was a plea in her voice. 'We are *very* near now, and there *will* be warmth.' The words slurred, and carried little conviction. Lidi shook her black mop again.

'No! *You* go. I will wait here, and go to sleep. You will come back with food for me, in a little while.' She made as if to lie down in the soft, deadly snow. Ela bent, taking her by the thin shoulders, shaking.

'Lidi! You cannot sleep. If you sleep now, it will be for ever!' The head shook, but still the eyelids drooped. 'Lidi! Mow is waiting! At the raft. So alone, without you. Come on, Lidi. Come on!' The big eyes were shiny slits below heavy lids. Lidi was letting herself sink into that soft, desirable warmth at the back of her mind: but the small mouth moved, cracked lips struggled with the shape, and from far back in the fuzzy warm Lidi murmured, 'Mow.'

'Mow!' cried Ela, shaking the child's limp frame. 'Mow! Mow! Mow!'

The warm was going away. She was sitting in something cold. Her hands hurt. Her head snapped back and forth on its slender neck. She bit her tongue, tasting salt. The light hurt her eyes. She screwed them up, then opened them. The shaking stopped. Ela's face, with beads of sweat, was close to her own. Warm feathers of breath.

'Get up, Lidi! Up. Get up.'

'My tongue hurts.'

Another brief shake.

'Never mind your tongue. Stand up. Stand up, now!'

Her legs wouldn't move.

'My legs won't move.'

Ela's big hands, chafing.

'Ow!'

Ela, panting, chafing the blue little legs.

'Ow . . . you hurt me! Oooow!'

Lidi kicked out, angry. Ela leapt back.

'Your legs move *now*!' she panted, triumphant.

Lidi rose, reeling, and recovered herself. Her blue legs were tinged with pink.

'You *hurt* me! You *skinned* me like a bear!' she screeched.

Ela laughed through her tiredness.

'I got you up again, Lidi, that's all.' She held out her hand to the child. 'Come on.'

A cold stiff hand crept into hers, and she turned her face north, and froze. A man stood among the boles, looking at them. His bow was in his hand. Lidi saw, and made a small cry, moving to stand behind Ela's legs. The man came forward, slowly. He walked like a man in a dream. His face was thin under the raggy beard. Ela gazed into the gaunt face, and she lurched forward, dragging Lidi.

'Modd!'

The man nodded, dazedly. His eyes were blank, but recognition struggled there.

'Ela . . . and Lidi,' he croaked.

Ela threw her arms about the skinny neck. The man tottered, almost falling from her weight. She disengaged, stepping back.

'I am sorry . . . you are sick?' Her eyes searched his face.

'Hungry,' he said huskily. 'We starve. Better you stayed with Gawl.'

Something occurred to him.

'You come through the *night?*'

Ela nodded.

'Yes. The bead protected us.' She held up the bead. Modd looked at it.

'I remember the bead,' he said, thickly. 'But we starve here. The bead will bring no food; no fire.' There was hopelessness in his voice. Ela let go of Lidi's hand, and took the small bundle from her waist.

'These will bring food, Modd,' she said. 'Hold out your hand.'

The hunter did so, and Ela opened her bundle, and spilled a small pile of arrowheads and spear tips into the shaking hand. Modd looked at them, and his features creased into a smile, and he cried out with joy and relief, 'It is *good* you come here with weapons to save your people!'

Ela looked into his eyes, anxious.

'Are the people living, all of them?' she asked.

The hunter nodded.

'All living, though they are weak and sick, and could not have lived much longer.'

He stooped, gathering the weary Lidi into his thin arms.

'Come; we will go to them.'

It was as much as he could do to carry the child, but he would not give her to Ela, so the girl walked beside him, carrying his bow, and the precious flints.

'We saw no smoke for many days,' said Ela.

Modd shook his head.

'There has been no fire.' And, as the pair trudged along, and Lidi slept in the warrior's arms, he told Ela how, after the flint gathering expedition failed, the people had gradually used up the flint they had already. Sometimes an arrow would miss its target, and be lost among the trees. Now and then a wounded animal would carry a spear tip in its body. 'Soon,' he told her, 'we had only the bone points and the sharpened sticks. We could no longer hunt the *big* creatures, and had to live on fishes and hares, and roots. Then it grew colder. The lake froze. The ground became hard, so that the women could not dig for roots, and the small creatures went away. We ate bark from the trees, and the soft inside of the reeds, and each day we grew weaker. Once a flock of birds came to the lake, and walked on the ice, and Morg shot one with his bow and a wooden arrow, but there was meat enough only for Mow and Cyl. Even the birds were hungry and this one was very thin.'

Modd paused in his tale, shaking his grizzled head at the memory. Ela's heart had warmed at his mention of Morg. Morg, who had brought meat to the children when there had been none for so long.

'Gyre,' she told herself bitterly, 'would have missed the bird, or if he had hit it, he would have sneaked off to eat it all himself.' Modd stopped, shifting the limp infant on to his thin shoulder, before resuming his slow trudge, and his story.

'Day after day, the three of us – Daf, Morg, and me – went out with our bows, but, as I have said, the cold had driven away all the small creatures. Only the elk and the buffalo remained. We tried to dig a pit, to catch a buffalo, but we could only scratch the hard earth, with our antler picks. Then one day, our hunger and the cries of the children drove us to foolishness. We attacked an old bull buffalo. Daf and Morg had bone-tip spears, and I had my bow, and some arrows of sharpened wood.'

Ela looked at the feeble man.

'What happened?' she asked, anxiously.

'We came upon him stripping bark from a birch,' answered Modd, in a tired voice. 'I shot an arrow, aiming at his eye. I missed. The buffalo has a very small eye,' he said, defensively. 'The arrow just bounced off his skull.'

'What happened then?' asked Ela.

'The buffalo turned to face us. Morg ran in, and thrust his spear at its side, but it barely pierced the hide, and Morg was thrown to the ground.'

Ela's eyes widened.

'Was he hurt – did the buffalo gore him?' she asked, rapidly. Modd shook his head.

'It *would* have gored him, but Daf ran in, and thrust his spear at its snout. The buffalo turned on Daf, lunging with its great head, and one horn caught him in the side. Then the creature was gone, crashing away with blood streaming from its snout. Morg was not hurt, and we carried Daf home. He lies there still, and his wound is slow to heal.'

Modd seemed disinclined to proceed further with his narrative, and when Ela glanced at him, to discover the reason for his pause, his face wore a far-away look, and a frown sat between his misty eyes. The girl said nothing, and the pair slogged on in silence for a while. They had rounded the northern end of the lake now, and were moving southwest towards the platform. Sometimes, where the forest was thin, Ela caught glimpses of the frozen lake away to her left. A pale sun hung low in the same direction, and its wan light made the ice look more cold, somehow, than it really was.

Presently, Modd began to speak again, in a low voice.

'After Daf was hurt, we held a council. The chief said that because the women and children were dying, he would send word to Gawl, inviting him to return as chief, if he would bring flint.'

Ela gasped.

'No! Not Gawl! But no word came to him – what happened?'

Modd smiled grimly, and said, 'The women told the old man that they would sooner die, and their children also.'

Ela smiled.

'It is good! Why, Gawl cannot lead wisely, and now his followers *know* that he cannot. My father knows this, but Gawl rages and threatens, and they are all afraid. He is like a wounded buffalo.'

Modd grunted.

'I think that the chief was glad, in his heart, when the women chose as they did. But it is no small thing to die with hunger. Soon, we had no dry wood for the fire, and had not the strength left to cut more. We burned reeds and bark, and one night, when Morg was tending the flames, he was overcome with hunger, and fell down. When he awoke, the fire was out.' The thin hunter shrugged, a resigned expression on his gaunt face. 'There was no fire in our lamps, because the children had eaten the fat from them. We sat each night, all together in my hut, because mine is in the middle of the platform. And with no flame to keep them away, the lost ones drew nearer and nearer each night. We could hear them, calling to us in the dark, and we were afraid.'

A picture came to Ela's mind of the frightened people, huddled in the flimsy hut, and in her head she heard the cold thin keening through invisible trees, and she shuddered.

'In the night that is just gone,' continued Modd, 'Daf became very sick, and Morg chewed bark for him so that he might swallow. And I came into the forest to seek food that is not here.' He sighed, heavily, 'It would have been the last time.'

Ela gazed at the tired man, concern in her eyes.

'Have you strength enough to hunt again, you and Morg?' she asked, 'Now that there is flint?'

Modd laughed, briefly.

'Ha! There will be a fine elk today. We will find the strength, and tonight we will light lamps to see our children's bellies grow tight with meat. You have saved all of your people, Ela.'

The trees thinned. Ela could see the platform, silent under snow. The birches here had no bark: they stood white and dying. They came out of the trees, this weary couple, with the sleeping child, and slithered down the bare slope to the reedy edge of the platform. No voices were raised in welcome, and no smoke hung on the frigid sky, but, although she was almost dead from weariness and cold, Ela felt a lightness in her breast that told her she had come home.

7

Trond was dreaming. It was spring, and the reeds were putting up their tender green spikes to fringe the platform. The ice was gone, and in the warm lake, fish were mating and spawning. In the reed beds, birds were building, and he knew them by their calls, though he could not see them. The grebe was back, and the bittern, and the moorhen. The sun was stronger, and higher in the sky. And when he looked landward, the forest was hazy with buds. The hunting was easy, and the round-bellied people were preparing for their springtime trek into the teeming hills. Their chatter bubbled lightly on the mild air. He was sitting at the platform edge, with his fish-spear, and beside him lay a great pile of flashing, quivering fishes. Another fish swam lazily beneath his poised barb, and he watched it, without striking. He had so many fishes already. He was warm, and full, and sleepy. The ripples made sun-patterns on the sandy bed, and they drew his mind away, so that his head nodded emptily, like a moon-flower. And he drooped beside his dying fire, and dreamed this dream, as dawn washed cold and slow over the frigid cliff top; and the ache in his belly was stilled, and he smiled.

In her dim lodge; Reda half-woke; threw out one arm, patting the earthen floor for the child's body. Through her sleep-mist, she knew the not-thereness of Lidi, and sat up, startled. Her eyes swept the half-darkness, quickly, fearful. Not there. Swiftly, on her knees, she emerged into the dawn, the child's name on her lips. The camp lay still. Only 'Lidi', twice, sharply, broke the silence.

The dream melted, and Trond came into his cold, stiff body. The platform was gone away, and the spring was not yet born, and the remembering made him groan as he lifted his head to the sound. The woman saw him; saw that he had been sleeping. She stood, and came to him.

'Lidi,' she said, anxious. 'Where is Lidi?'

Trond shook his head, muttering.

'I do not know: I have not seen her. Is she not sleeping?'

Reda snorted, impatient.

'If she was sleeping, would I ask you where she is?'

And she turned, ducking back into the hut, to wake Alpa. Angry, frightened sounds came out of the hut. Trond groaned again, and stood up. There would be trouble. He had slept. The woman had seen him. The fire was nearly out, and Lidi was missing. He pushed a mound of twigs into the fire with his foot, abstractedly. They crackled, and smoke curled up. He glanced around. Save for the three houses, the cliff top was empty. An even snow-cover lay overall. The forest began abruptly, black. Alpa came out with his spear, and Reda followed. Alpa called.

'Trond! Did you see the child? Have you seen anything in the night?'

'I have seen nothing,' said Trond, and, 'He was sleeping,' accused Reda.

There was a stirring in Gawl's hut, and the leader stuck out his head.

'What is wrong?' he growled. 'Can I not sleep in peace any longer?'

'It is Lidi!' cried Reda. 'She is not here. Is she with you?'

Gawl snorted.

'Why should she be with me?' and he pulled his head back into the darkness, muttering.

Inside, Pab began to squawk. Reda, almost crying, ran to Trond's hut, calling to Hila, who put out her head.

'Lidi! Is she with you?' cried Reda, grasping at this final hope. Hila withdrew her head to look, and stuck it out again, and her expression was one of terror.

'Ela is not here!' she cried. 'There is nobody!'

'They are gone!' wailed Reda, wringing her cold hands. 'They are nowhere.'

Hila crawled out, and stood up.

'There is snow,' she said. 'Are there no tracks?'

Alpa ran towards his own hut, his eyes on the snow. Gawl came out, clutching his robe tight about him, and still muttering. Alpa gave a cry.

'Here are tracks; but faint. It snowed after.' The

people moved over to see. Gawl bent, examining the almost obliterated marks.

'Lidi went long ago,' he pronounced, 'when the night was new. Trond! You were watching. What did you see in the night?'

Trond groaned inwardly.

'I saw nothing,' he muttered, sullen.

He had come to hate his leader, and to fear his temper.

'He was sleeping!' cried Reda, bitterly.

'I was sleeping,' growled Trond, 'a little.'

Hila wailed.

'A little? Your own daughter walked away in the night, with Lidi, and you saw nothing. A little?'

Gawl glowered at Trond.

'When there is time, you will be punished for this,' he promised, grimly. Something occurred to him. His scowl became blacker, and his voice rose, shrilly. 'Ela! She has gone because she is promised to my son. Where are her tracks? She will be found, and punished.' He cast around in the snow, near Trond's hut. 'She has left no tracks!' he screamed. 'She has gone without making tracks!' He was frantic in his rage.

'No!' cried the calmer Alpa. 'That is not possible. Do you not see what it means?' He glanced around. Nobody spoke. 'It means that Ela went away *before* Lidi, and the snow filled up her tracks. They did not go together!'

Reda checked her weeping.

'Not together?' she choked. 'Then why Lidi? Ela had reason, but not Lidi; not my Lidi!'

Gawl turned on the distraught woman.

'Reason?' he screamed. 'What reason? To be the woman of the chief; is this not an honour?'

Reda dropped her eyes, confused, and recommenced her crying.

Hila said, 'She was promised to Morg.'

Gawl laughed, near hysteria.

'Morg is dead. They are *all* dead!'

Gyre, awakened by the noise, had emerged in time to hear the discovery of Ela's absence. He stood beside Gawl, scowling peevishly.

'She thinks he is alive,' he said. 'She believes he can live without food, or do *anything*. She thinks he is greater than the lost ones. That is where she is gone: to the platform!'

A fresh burst of crying came from Reda.

'Lidi,' she sobbed. 'Why would *Lidi* go there? Where would *she* go in the night?'

Trond muttered sulkily.

'Lidi left tracks. Why do we not follow?'

'She will be gone to the lost ones, and my Ela, also,' cried Hila.

'It is too late. You slept, and it is too late!' And she turned away, and stood gazing at the forest through her tears.

Reda shook her tangled head, emphatically.

'No! Follow. Lidi has the bead.'

A sharp, scoffing noise burst from Gyre.

'The bead! What good is a bead in the night?'

The distraught woman turned on him, her face a mixture of anger and desperation.

'She came back before. With Morg. Because she had

the bead. She was in the forest, in the night. And she came back.'

Gyre cast her a scornful look. Her anguish did not touch him. He could feel only his anger against Ela, and his hatred of Morg. He made no reply, but scoffed again, turned on his heels, and went up towards the cliff. Reda turned to Gawl.

'You are our leader. Give orders. Have the tracks followed.'

Gawl looked at the tearstained face, and then dropped his eyes. His anger had cooled. He looked uneasy.

'It is as Hila says,' he muttered. 'It is too late.'

'Then I will go by myself!' cried Reda.

Alpa took her arm, and looked at his leader.

'Reda and I. We *must* go,' he said quietly.

'I will go also,' said Trond, 'to seek my daughter.'

'No! Alpa and Reda shall go. You shall stay, Trond,' snapped Gawl.

'But why?' cried Trond. 'It is *I* who slept, so that they went away. And my daughter . . .'

'No!' It was almost a scream. Gawl's fists were clenched, his teeth bared. 'You will stay here. You are not to be trusted. You might not return . . .' His voice trailed off, and he looked confused. He glanced round, to see if anybody else had heard. Gyre was out of earshot, sitting on the cliff edge. Hila was leaning on a hut, her head buried in her arms and Jodi was trying to comfort her.

Trond saw his confusion, and said, 'Return? How could I not return? Where would I go, when darkness came?'

Gawl shook his head. Then his face darkened, and instead of answering, he roared, 'You will stay because *I* have spoken! I am your leader!'

Trond became angry, and his anger lent him courage.

'You told us that the others are all dead, and you do not believe it yourself: you are afraid that we will go to the platform,' he cried.

Gawl turned purple with fury.

'Not "*we*"!' he screeched. 'Not "we": just *you*, because you are a fool. Of course they are dead: there has been no smoke. Alpa and Reda *know* they are dead. They will return. But *you* are a fool, and your *daughter* is a fool, and you would both sooner die with the other fools than stay here where you can have full bellies!' He stood up very close to Trond, and thrust his purple face into the other man's. 'And I tell you this,' he hissed. 'If I did not need your spear when we hunt, I would say to you, *"Go: die with the other fools!"* But you will stay, because that is my command!'

Trond stood his ground for a moment, trembling with rage; then his courage ebbed, and he wilted, turned, and slunk away towards Hila. Gawl looked scornfully after him, then turned to the waiting group.

'Go,' he said. 'Follow the tracks. Be sure to leave time enough to return before night. If you lose the trail, return at once.'

Alpa put an arm around Reda.

'Come,' he said.

They moved away downhill, following the faint tracks.

'Lidi has the bead,' said Reda, mechanically.

Gawl watched them go, until he lost them among the trees.

Gyre kicked at the white stone with his cold heel until he kicked it free, and it went skittering down the cliff in a shower of dirt. He gazed out across the dull ice-lake. They were dead. *He* was dead. A picture of Morg's face came to him, and the hatred burned. He was dead. He *must* be dead, by now. And Ela, also. Gone to the lost ones, because she would not come to him. He did not feel sorry for her. He felt angry, and satisfied, at the same time. Angry, because she had chosen death rather than life as his woman; satisfied, because she had met the fate she deserved, and Morg would never have her now. 'If you had become my woman,' he told the picture of her, which now floated before his eyes, 'the best part of it all, for me, would have been to know that I had taken you away from Morg. And now the night has done that for me.'

And he smiled faintly in his reverie. Behind him, his mother crouched in her doorway, cooking meat. His father had retired to his bed of skins again, to brood. He spent a lot of his time brooding now. And Jodi was silent, too; hardly speaking either to her man, or to her son.

'It is the cold,' Gyre told himself. 'When it is warm again, the people will be happy, in the hills.' And he thought a little about the happiness in the hills. It would all be so again; and this time, there would be no Morg to strut among them, feeling himself to be greater than they. Gyre felt a warm glow, which almost smothered the small voice in his head, murmuring,

'And no Ela, and Lidi. No Mow, and no Cyl. No . . .' The boy shook his head, to make the pictures go away. Pictures of children who ran across the grassy slope in the sun-warm hills. And then the children went away, and there was just the grassy slope. The quiet, grassy, slope. Gyre sat a long time, seeing that slope, along with its sun-warm grass, and its quiet. The unbroken grey of the sky was reflected dully in the ice-sheet of the lake, so that there was only this greyness before his far-away eyes, and nothing to distract him, as he peered forward into a desolate time. Ela and Lidi were dead. The platform people were dead, also. There was Gawl. And Jodi and Pab. Alpa, Reda, Trond and Hila. And himself. The people. The new lords of the forest.

'When Gawl grows old, then I shall be the leader; the chief,' he told himself, and the voice inside his head said, quietly: 'When Gawl grows old, then Alpa will be old, also. And Trond, and Reda and Hila. There will be myself and Pab, to hunt for the old people. For the old people.' He shook his head again, realising that he had spoken aloud. Old people. If there were no more children for Reda or Hila, then one day there would be only old people. And after that. What he saw after that numbed his mind, as his dangling feet were numbed by the cold. To be the last of the people. To be alone. To die, and to leave the forest to the wolves, and the birds, and the winds.

At the blurred line where the ice became the sky, a smudge of dark appeared. So faint was it that, though the boy's eyes saw it, it did not impinge on his consciousness.

The smudge became a stain, and the stain spread

slowly up the heavy sky, breaking up Gyre's vision-field of uniform grey. And the numbing greyness in his head broke, too, so that he saw with his mind, as well as with his eyes: and his mind said 'smoke'. His lips said 'smoke', too, as he scrambled to his feet, clumsily, because of the numbness. Then he was running down the slope, shouting. Like the day the dugout had come to the flint-digging; except that now the emotions he was feeling were very different. Gawl crawled out of his hut, muttering, 'Smoke? What smoke?'

He cast bleary eyes westward, and saw. His jaw dropped, momentarily. Then he recovered himself; his mouth set firmly, and he scowled, and strode up the slope to the cliff top, where the others were already gathered, pointing and chattering, in their excitement. As Gawl came up, Trond was saying, 'He told us they were dead, and they are not. See; it is as I said.'

And they all gazed across at the distant smoke; Hila nodded agreement.

Gawl burst among them, shouting.

'They are *not* alive! It is Ela. She has made a fire on the platform.'

Hila said, 'I would be happy to believe that; for it would mean my daughter is at least *alive*.'

'I think that *some* of the others are alive, at least,' said Trond.

Gawl rounded on him.

'Your head is full of thistlefur,' he snarled. 'You *cannot* think. They banished us for ever: even if they *were* alive, they would *kill* your daughter for going back; and Lidi, also!'

'How can we tell?' asked Jodi, quietly. 'They have, perhaps, *done* this.'

Gawl reddened, and his voice rose with his fury.

'Then why do they make fire today, after many days without? Perhaps you think they will *cook* the children, having killed them! I tell you, it is Ela. She will be brought back, and punished.'

Gyre heard little of this. He stood, a little way apart, looking vacantly across the dull ice, trying to sort out his feelings. The platform people were enemies. It was a bad thing, to see their fires. He knew this; but he could not feel it. He had seen pictures of what might be: of the people, dying one by one; and of the forest without the people: the forest, going on and on, without anybody to know about it. As though there never had been the people. And the trees and the rain and all the timid things would go on; there never would be people again, but it would make no difference to anything. And suddenly it had become very important to Gyre that there should be people: not that there should be *Gyre*; but that there should always be people; *any* people. *Any* people was better than *no* people; better than the quiet that would go on for ever. And now there was the smoke; and the smoke hung on the air like a great, tapered finger that pointed to a place where men might be found. And Gyre looked at the smoke of his enemies, and it seemed to him like the smoke of his friends.

The people watched for a little, then dispersed, quietly; each with his own thoughts; and wandered down the slope. Gawl continued to mutter that it was Ela's fire;

that the platform people were dead. The faces of his people were blank, or averted, and he seemed to feel his power slipping away. Even Gyre had looked at him strangely just now.

As the straggle of people reached the hut area, there came a hail from the forest fringe, and Alpa and Reda came out of the trees, and began to mount the slope. Alpa was carrying something in his hands. The people waited in the space between the huts, near to the low fire. The exhausted hunter came panting up, and threw down the two grass dolls on the trodden snow.

'We found these. They stood beside the track, and pointed to the platform. Ela and Lidi are together, and have gone to the platform.' Hila sighed her relief.

Reda said, 'Lidi has the bead. It kept them from the lost ones.'

Gawl seized his opportunity.

'It is as I said!' he cried, spreading his arms wide, and turning round slowly to look at all the people. 'The fire is Ela's fire. Tomorrow, we will go to the platform, and bring her back, and Lidi, also.'

'No!' Reda had come wearily up, behind her man, and spoke, resignedly. 'We cannot go there. The people are alive. Our children have gone back to the people.'

At once, excited chatter broke out, so that Gawl was forced to shout his question at the woman.

'How do you know this?' he rapped. 'You have not been away long enough to have been at the platform.'

Reda shook her head.

'We were not at the platform. We followed the track

for a little, where the dolls pointed. We came to a place where the children's tracks met a man's tracks, in the snow. We do not know what man. The tracks lead towards the platform. Ela carried Lidi. We saw smoke, and turned back.'

Hila was crying softly, and Reda moved to comfort her.

'I will never see Ela again,' sobbed the mother, 'but I am glad she is safe, and with the people.'

Everybody was talking, except Gyre, who stood quietly listening. Gawl cried out, angrily.

'Do not talk of the people! There may be only one; the man they met in the forest. And they can do nothing without flints: the winter has far to go, and they cannot hunt without weapons. All will die!' At this, the hubbub died down. Gawl was right; the two children had left, only to starve among the platform people. The angry leader glared at his followers; outwardly arrogant, inwardly relieved that he was still able to subdue them. He was about to rant at them further, when the abject figure of Trond came forward. His face was pale, and he looked shaken. His voice quavered, as he said, 'My weapons; my pouch of flint heads . . . it is gone! Ela must have taken it away.'

8

A cold wind whipped spitefully across the lake, as Morg ducked through the doorway of his father's hut, and stood gazing eastwards to the frigid dawn. He leaned his spear against the wall for a moment, pulling the bearskin cloak more closely about his lean brown shoulders.

Across the platform, close to the choppy green fringe of the lake, the chief's hut stood in darkness still, but Morg knew that soon Tilde would wake and emerge sleepily into the dim light, to take from the smouldering heap of last night's fire a glowing stick with which to kindle her lamp. Then it would be almost time.

Morg glanced round as his father, grunting, emerged from their hut, his long grey hair lashed like sleet into his creased face by the wind.

'You rise early, my son,' the old man said. His voice was gruff, but there was gentleness there, and pride. 'See, the sun has not yet risen to light the lamp upon the day of your manhood.'

Morg shook his head, so that his black hair brushed the brown fur of the bearskin.

'I could not sleep longer, Father,' he replied. 'I have waited too long for this day.'

Old Daf laid a scarred, blunt hand on his son's shoulder.

'Take care, Morg,' he grunted. 'Let not your eagerness become carelessness. The winter is hard, and a hungry bear is a swift bear.'

Morg gripped the shaft of his spear, liking the smooth feel of the weapon he had made for himself.

He had cut, from a hazel beside the lake, the straightest shaft he could find, and had stripped away the soft bark with a scraper of flint. Then, using the axe of his father, with its polished stone head, he had split the narrower end of the shaft, making a deep notch, into which he had fitted the long, slender point of white flint which had taken him so long to shape. It was a good point. Even Old Gart had admired it, testing the edge with his gnarled, horny thumb. The other children had stood, watching Morg as he chipped away at this flint, shaping it, flake by flake. And they had known that, when the task was finished, when the edge was sharp, their friend would be one of them no longer; for with this spear, Morg would prove himself a man. He had fixed point to shaft firmly, binding the split with thongs of deer hide, soaked to make them tight, and had rubbed into them the fragrant sticky resin of the birch tree, until he had a weapon as fine as any owned by the hunters.

Now he gripped his spear, and thought of the bear. Like his father before him, like all hunters, Morg must go alone into the forest, and there face in combat a great brown bear. Using only the spear and the skinning knife, he must kill his bear, and return to the village with its skin and its head. The skin would one day be worn by his son, even as he was now wearing the skin of Daf's first bear. The head would be stuck on a sharpened pole, outside his father's hut, to be a source of pride to him as he grew old. And when these things were done, then Morg would be a hunter, and a man.

While Morg thought of these things, Tilde came, to take the glowing twig into her man's hut, and kindle the lamp, touching the hot faggot to a scrap of deer skin floating in its stone bowl of pig's fat. Soon now the chief would be ready to receive him.

Morg stood beside his father, and both waited. Daf's thoughts were of the day long ago when he had set out from another village in the dawn, to face his bear. He had returned as a man; Morg now wore the skin, and the great white skull snarled silently on the apex of his hut's roof. He had also returned with an arm which was opened from shoulder to wrist by a slash of the beast's great claws. The scars had remained permanently.

The doorway of the chief's hut now flickered with yellow light. Tilde came and sat outside, mixing food in a stone quern. There was a stirring in Daf's hut, and Morg's mother emerged, shivering. She had slept badly, her thoughts ever turning to her poor brother, who had walked away into a dawn of long ago to seek his bear, and had never returned. Morg saw his mother's worried face, and smiled.

'Have no fear, Mother!' he said softly. 'When I am a man I will journey to the sea, and bring you amber and shells for your hair.'

'May it be,' murmured the woman.

Daf put his huge arm around her shoulders.

'Woman, you are the wife of a great hunter, and today you will be the mother of another. What ails thee?'

'My brother set out on such a day as this,' she sighed, 'and we never saw him again!'

'Your brother was not a strong boy, and he had a twisted foot,' said Daf. 'Look at Morg – he's almost as tall as I am!'

The village was awakening. As the first thin rays of the sun came weakly over the lake, to wash the naked birches behind the village, the women appeared, taking hot sticks to light their lamps, and preparing food. On any ordinary morning, the children would have been off now, out of the village, to spear small fish or to dig with their antler picks in the hard ground for edible roots. Today, nobody left the platform for all would see the setting out of Morg on his proving hunt.

There came the sound of movement from within the chief's hut, and everybody turned towards the sound. Momentarily, the bright doorway was obscured by a crouching figure, which unfolded slowly, until the chief stood, erect and tall, his ceremonial robes of wolf skin sweeping to the ground. His proud head bore the head-dress of antlers. He stood for a moment, silhouetted against the bleak dawn. Then he raised his right arm and beckoned, silently commanding Morg to advance. A murmured 'ah!' from the assembled villagers, as Morg detached himself from his parents, and gripping his spear, walked steadily, to stand before his chief. Morg was a tall boy, yet the old, wise chief gazed down upon him from a great height. At first he did not speak, and Morg gazed steadily into the shrewd eyes, his body erect, his spear haft vertical beside him. All the villagers had now abandoned their tasks, and had arranged themselves in a half-circle around the group which consisted of the chief, Morg himself, Tilde, and Daf, who was holding out his own skinning knife towards the chief. The great man took the knife, and, with a deer-hide thong, fastened it round Morg's waist. At a signal from her man, Tilde stepped forward with her pot of red, sticky fluid, and handed it to him. Dipping a long, thick finger into the pot, the chief drew upon Morg's cheeks four bars of colour, two on each side of his nose. As he did so, he intoned in a solemn voice:

'Morg, son of Daf, the time of your testing is come: you are a child no longer. Go now, and return as a man, or do not return.'

Morg lifted his right hand, so that the spear stood vertically before his face. The pale sun glistened wetly in the pigment, and threw the shadow of the spear haft down the line of his nose, and his face took on, momentarily, the aspect of a hideous mask. Then, without having uttered a word, Morg turned his back upon his chief, and upon his father, and strode silently across the compound, his shadow long before him.

Mow and Lidi sat in the shadow of Modd's hut, and watched him as he went. Mow, already impatient to be after his own first bear, watched with a fierce expression, and made vicious stabbing motions at the ground between his feet with his slender fish-spear. Lidi, merely a girl, watched with the stoic resignation expected of a woman in the matter of men's affairs. Since her return to the platform, Lidi had lived with Mow in his father's hut; the companion she had longed for at the cliff was now virtually a brother to her. He was grown strong again, after his long hunger, and the two played together contentedly, so that, when Lidi did sometimes think of her mother, it was fleetingly, and without pain. Ela sat before the chief's hut, where she had found a home with Tilde. Lately, it seemed to Mow and Lidi, she had stopped being a girl, and was concentrating very hard on becoming a woman. Lidi went to watch her sometimes, and seeing the set expression on her face, and the little frown marks between her eyes, it became plain to the child that it was no small thing, to become a woman.

Ela spent most of her time now sitting in front of Tilde's hut, while Tilde instructed her in the tasks which a woman must perform in order to run her home. Ela was learning that these tasks were far more difficult than the practised ease of the grown women made them look, and much less interesting than she had thought they would be. Today she was preparing a wolf skin for making into a robe. This she was doing by taking small sections at a time into her mouth, and chewing the stiff hide until it became soft and pliable, then working it in her fingers to a permanent softness. She was bored, and her fingers and jaws ached, so, as she worked, she was making believe that she was the woman of a great hunter, who had killed a wolf with his bare hands, and brought her the skin, so that she should have a warm robe when the snows came.

As Morg strode through the village, Ela watched

him with her eyes, while keeping her head bent over her work. He walked swiftly, and his eyes looked straight ahead, but as he came opposite to where she sat, he turned his head, and stared right at her. She dropped her eyes at once, and her cheeks felt fiery. Morg passed by, and Ela followed him with her eyes.

'Morg will be a very great hunter one day,' she thought. She continued to watch him until, at a sharp word from Tilde, she caught up her work, and went quickly inside the hut.

Morg covered the ground quickly as he left the settlement behind, padding quietly between the trees, his bare feet making little sound upon the carpet of fallen leaves. The forest swam in a dim, misty light, and a dank odour arose from the dewy ground.

Once, when Morg was a small boy, a bear had come into the village, seeking food scraps. The hunters had surrounded it, stabbing and goading it with their spears. Suddenly, as little Morg had watched it, it had reared up on its hind legs, so that it stood a head taller than the chief himself, and had broken through the ring of men, bowling them over like reeds before the knife, to shamble off, growling, into the forest, trailing a long spear haft whose point had penetrated its shaggy side. The spear, Morg now remembered, had not even slowed the great beast down. He thought of the words of the hunters, which he had heard as they retold the stories of their hunting by the flickering fire in the night-shrouded settlement:

'The bear has a hard body, and a thick coat. He must be speared through the muzzle, or in the mouth, or in the soft belly. But to do any of these things, a hunter must be very close – a thrown spear will not find its mark.'

'Very close!' thought Morg.

He saw in his mind the scars on his father's arm. The bear whose skin he now wore had inflicted those wounds with a spear in its mouth, and a skinning knife had finished the affair. A skinning knife driven with the left hand into the bear's neck by old Daf, as he lay wounded under the huge, pain-maddened beast. Morg gripped his spear tighter, his left hand feeling for the knife of flint at his waist as he strode along. Morg knew where he was going, though he had never travelled so far from the village before. He knew that, if he kept the sun at his back, and travelled quickly, he would reach his destination with time left to find his bear and fight with it, and return to the settlement by nightfall. The place he sought was a bare, rock-strewn hillside, which led up to the foot of a sheer, limestone cliff, which was pitted with cave entrances. In winter, the bears spent most of their time in these caves, driven out from time to time by hunger. It was here that generations of hunters of Morg's clan had come to challenge the bears, and to prove their manhood. More than one, Morg knew, had left his bones to whiten on that rocky hillside. Presently the ground over which he was moving began to slope upwards, and grey, lichen-covered boulders lay, half buried, between the trees. The birches thinned, and ahead Morg could see an open slope, treeless and rocky, with tufts of coarse grass and clumps of ling and blueberry. He slowed, and, spear at the ready, advanced cautiously, gliding soundlessly over the forest floor until he stood in the fringe of the forest. Here Morg paused, his body moulded against a silvery trunk, so that the shadows of trees, falling across him, broke his outline, and he became almost invisible. He raised his head, his nostrils quivering as he searched the air. The scent of bear came to him. The breeze blew softly down the hill, from the chalky cliff. It would carry no warning of his presence to the bears.

The sun was now high over Morg's shoulder. Soon, it would begin its long slide down the pale sky to the black forests of the west. Screwing up his eyes, against the light, Morg searched the broken ground between himself and the foot of the cliff. Mottled landscape, white boulders dotted with grey lichen, dark rock-shadows splashed over sere ling clumps, grasses shivering in the wind. Cloud-shadow moving rapidly downhill, dimming the slope briefly, then sliding on. Feeble sunlight washing streakily down the pale cliff, picking out in black the fissures, ledges and caves that pitted its face. No other movement. No sound, save the softly sighing birches.

The boy moved, running crouched towards a boulder halfway up the slope. In its shadow he paused, watchful, listening. Nothing. Fear mounted as though feeding upon the very absence of anything to fear. Despite the cold, sweat trickled from beneath the matted hair on the brow, forming funnels in the red pigment daubs on the cheeks. Lips parted, teeth glinting in a half snarl, breath hissing. Watchful. Tensed, like a sapling bent for a snare. Above, and now only a little way ahead, the cliff, and two caves;

one narrow and high, a crack in the cliff face; the other low and wide, with a flattened area of short grass before it. The low cave. It must be right. Grass trodden down.

Morg moved forward, a liquid motion between boulder and boulder; like oil oozing uphill. A spear's cast from the cave he stopped, shoulder pressed to the cold, rough surface of a man-high rock. Listen. Breeze making a faint, hollow sound around the cave mouth. Somewhere within, water dripping. Morg, crouching, eyes searching the hard ground ahead, saw marks in the beaten grass. Bear tracks. The scent, also, was stronger here.

His limbs quivered. Fear like a sickness swept his body. Voices echoing inside his head: 'Go, melt back in the forest. Get away. Return not to the village, but journey on, to a place where no bears roam. To the west where, the old men say, there is no night. Then Morg saw his father, standing near his hut in the dusk, gazing to the west, and from within he thought he heard the soft crying of his mother. And little Mow was there, leaning on his fish-spear, and Ela, working at her wolf skin. And later, when night came, they would all sit near to the fire, and listen to the sounds out there beyond the glow and when the wind came moaning in the trees, and the rain like unseen weeping in the night, then his mother would believe that he was there, in the fringes of the trees, weeping with the other lost ones, because lost ones cannot approach the fires of the living, and must depart before dawn for the place where there is no day. And he shook himself, and tried the balance of his spear, and, bending quickly, lifted a crumbling lump of limestone. Hefting its weight with his left hand, Morg took aim, and sent the missile flashing into the cave mouth. A clattering, hollow sound, dying away into the cliff. Then nothing, save the drip, drip, of eternally falling water. Morg stepped into the open, away from the shadow of his rock, approaching the cave in a crouching run, spear rigid before him. Around the cave mouth there were bear tracks, and in the dust within. Inside the cave now, eyes screwing into the gloom. No movement. The boy scanned the walls on either side. The sun's weak light, penetrating a little way into the gloom, revealed green water-streaks, small ferns and mosses. A shift in the light: a deepening of the gloom: a sibilant, snuffling sound. Morg whirled. The bear, silhouetted in the cave mouth, was shuffling forward, its claws making little clicking sounds on the floor. Morg backed to the wall, spear pointed steadily at the great head with its tiny, red-rimmed eyes. The smell of the beast came to him, hot, and with the smell of carrion and hibernation. The bear was lean; a large male, and hungry. A soft growl, and the bear came, quickly. Jabbing wildly, twisting away, Morg scrabbled towards the cave mouth, bounded with a cry of fear into the clean open slope. Emerging, he whirled again, and the bear was with him. A thrust; the flint point jabbed into the black muzzle, and the bear reared towering; a roar, and a flailing paw knocked the spear aside. The bear lunged, and Morg felt the long claws flash through his hair. He skipped backwards, down the slope, lining up the spear again. Mouth gaping redly, the beast came in again. Morg jabbed desperately upwards, trying for a mouth-thrust, but the paws were up, protecting the head. Lightning fast he switched, dropping the spear to the exposed belly; his jab, too light, barely penetrated the skin, and the bear dropped on to four feet. Morg, still on the retreat, began to work sideways across the slope.

'I must be above him,' he gasped aloud. 'I cannot reach the head.'

Crabbing across the slope, keeping the spear rigidly pointed at the steadily advancing animal, he was level with the beast's position when his foot caught on a loose stone. Shifting his weight on to the foot, he fell; the bear rushed in. Morg raised his legs and lashed out at the great head. His heels smashed into the great wet muzzle, the head went up, and Morg's spear rammed into the exposed throat. Morg felt the solid impact, the flint sinking deeply, and, simultaneously, felt a tearing pain in his legs. His hold on the spear gone, he doubled up and rolled from beneath the descending mass of the bear. His roll brought him up against a rock, and he dragged himself into a sitting position, his torn legs splayed twistedly before him. The bear reared again, roaring, and flailing its huge paws at the spear haft, which now protruded loosely from under its slavering jaws. Morg hauled himself upright, his back against the rock. As he came erect, sickening pain swept him, and he almost fell. His thrust had not been a fatal one, and now he had no spear. The bear, which in its own pain had forgotten him, now shook its enormous head vigorously, and the spear came away, rattling among the rocks well down the slope. The bear's coat was streaked with blood below the wound, and when it roared, Morg could see that there was blood also inside its mouth: but it seemed unaffected, and came at him again. Throwing off his bear skin, Morg bounded naked down the slope, towards his weapon, grimacing against the pain in his legs. He threw himself forward, grabbed the spear, rolled, and came upright as the bear lunged at him again. He dodged, jabbed, and leapt up the slope. Now the animal was below him. The bear reared again, the blood shining darkly in its thick fur. Blood-flecked lips drawn back over long, yellow teeth, it moved up towards him, paws weaving before its face. Morg stood braced on his torn legs, wanting to retreat, but knowing that this time he must stand his ground. Spear gripped tightly with both hands, he waited. He was breathing heavily, and felt sick. He knew that he must finish this now, or die. The bear, having moved slowly to within ten feet of the exhausted boy, lunged forward and upwards, jaws agape, forepaws wide as if to embrace its victim. And Morg moved, not back, but forward, into that deadly embrace, flinging all his remaining strength into a mighty, two-handed thrust at the cavernous mouth. The point found its mark unerringly, and Morg, thrown off balance by the depth of the thrust, fell heavily, and rolled down the slope. Some way above him, the bear reared to its full height, and a horrible, gurgling roar rent the air. The spear haft protruded stiffly from the beast's mouth, and the huge paws flailed vainly at it. As Morg watched, the stricken creature toppled backwards, crashed to the ground, kicked once, and died. The terrible jaws gaped, and the spear haft pointed straight at the sky. Morg pulled himself erect. The pain in his legs was entirely submerged in another, joyful ache that came from deep within him. He strode up the hillside, to where his adversary lay broken and extinct. The sharp skinning knife was in his hand. He bent swiftly, and with a wrench, pulled free the bloody spear. The sun was sinking towards the west, and Morg, standing over the body of his victim, turned his face to the flaming sky, and raised his spear in exultant salute. The blood ran down the haft, along the upstretched arm, down the naked, sun-crimsoned side, to mingle with the blood that streaked the lean, swift leg, and the hills and forests rang to the victorious cry of the hunter.

9

The boughs sagged a little at the edge of the platform where Lidi was standing. The ice crackled among dead reeds, and here and there it splintered, so that water appeared between the blackened stumps of the boughs and the rotten grey ice. The wind came gently across the lake from the south, and all around the rim, winter was losing its grip on the shore. Heavy cloudbanks rolled north, weeping warm rains into the forest.

The child stood, looking eastwards across the flat greyness, but the misty rain came between, so that she could not see whether smoke rose on the far shore. Her sigh caused her brown shoulders to rise slowly, and then sag, quickly. Morg, crossing the platform with an armful of bark, saw the gesture and nodded his head slowly.

'The child wants its mother,' he told himself. 'And the same thing ails another.'

He ducked in through the doorway of the new lodge, and threw down his bark.

'Here is another lot,' he said.

Ela looked up from her work. Morg grinned, and motioned with his head towards the shore.

'Lidi is looking for her mother again,' he said.

Ela's smile was fragile.

'It is hurtful,' she said, softly, 'and not a thing for laughter.'

The boy's grin became a frown, and he squatted on his heels, looking at her across the lamp.

'I know,' he said. 'It is hurtful for Lidi, and it is hurtful also for you. But you would both be more unhappy, if you were with your people on the cliff.'

Ela nodded.

'We could never go back,' she whispered. 'But I want so much to see my mother again. I know that she is unhappy there, with Gawl, and she would run away if it were not for my father.'

Morg's frown deepened.

'Does your father still believe in Gawl?' he asked.

Ela shrugged.

'He is afraid of Gawl. He cannot oppose him, because Gawl might drive him away, and there is nowhere for him to go. He cannot return here. So he follows Gawl, and does what Gawl says. Gawl does not *need* the people's belief. They can turn to no other.'

'The women could come back,' said Morg. 'The chief has said so.'

'They will not leave their men,' replied the girl. Her voice softened. 'If you were with Gawl, I would stay with you.'

The boy smiled and nodded.

'I know,' he said.

He straightened up, and kicked the pile of bark with his toes.

'Melt the resin out of this today, Ela,' he said. 'Tomorrow, we make the dugouts ready. When the ice breaks, we must go again to the cliff for flint.' He paused in the doorway. 'I will speak with Gart,' he said, 'about Reda and your mother.'

He strode away over the boughs, towards the forest. Behind him, Lidi stood in the same place as before, and Mow stood beside her, disconsolate. He had wished so hard for her to come back to play with him, and now she hardly ever wanted to play at all. He kicked a twig into the slush, and gazed glumly into the mist.

When the sun sank into the trees, the chief went and sat by the fire in the middle of the platform, and called his people to come to him. Beside him sat Old Gart, like a heap of broken bones inside a skin. Both looked grave. When everyone was seated, the chief spoke to them.

'We have been pondering much, Gart and I, the question of flint and one other question.' He nodded his balding head towards Lidi, who sat between Mow and his mother. 'That other question concerns the child there.'

Lidi was startled by being thus spoken of by the chief, and dropped her eyes, shuffling a little closer to the woman.

'Lidi is cared for in the lodge of Modd,' continued the chief, 'and has all that we can give to her. But she wants her mother. Every day, I see her looking across the lake. We all have seen this.' There was a murmur of assent around the fire. 'Ela, also, I am told, is unhappy, because Hila cannot be here.' He paused, and rested his gaze slowly on each of his people in turn. 'The old man and myself have pondered much,' he repeated, 'and there is a way to help the children, which will also make it easy for us to have flint again.'

There was no sound. The firelight licked the attentive faces of the people, and fluttered in their eyes.

'We can send a man to the cliff,' continued the chief, 'to tell Gawl that he might return with all his people, if he swears that he will never again break the laws of the people.'

There were gasps in the twilight.

Modd said, 'But this would be most unwise. Gawl might swear, but who knows that he would live by his oath, for ever?'

Voices grunted agreement. Old Gart spoke, huskily.

'Gawl has caused his people to hate him. Now they see that he is a man of little wisdom, and of no kindness. They would not follow him again, and a man can do nothing alone.'

Nobody replied to this. Presently the chief said, 'It is a big thing. All the people must decide.'

Everyone looked into the fire, thinking. Morg said, 'Let them come back. I will carry the words to them.'

The four women looked at each other, and nodded. Tilde said, 'Let them come back.'

Daf frowned.

'There is danger in it,' he said. 'But there is wisdom.'

Modd spat into the fire. 'Kill the men; keep the women,' he growled.

Old Gart spoke sharply.

'You speak with the words of Gawl,' he said.

Modd shrugged. 'I see the foolishness of trusting them,' he replied, 'but I am alone. Do as the people wish.'

It was agreed. The people sat on, talking and warming themselves, until the haloed moon climbed out of the forest. Then in ones and twos they slipped away to their huts, until there was only Daf. And the warm wind took sparks from his fire, and blew them at the moon, which hurried on towards the dawn.

Jodi rammed her skinning knife into the soft place under the jaw, and drew it swiftly downwards with a sawing motion. The skin parted, and the entrails spilled out. Hila plunged her hands into the reeking pile, and pulled to free it from the carcass. Her arms were bloody to the elbows, and she knelt on crimson snow. Two butchered elk lay nearby. Reda was ripping back the open skin of one of these.

Outside Trond's hut, Alpa and Trond were mending spears. Gyre came down the slope with a skin of water, which he poured into the blackened pot on Jodi's fire. It was a clear day, and from the cliff top the boy had seen the smoke from the platform. As the water splashed into the pot, he wondered idly what was happening there today. The sight of smoke from their fires was enough to send Gawl into a rage, but Gyre drew a kind of comfort from it now: from its just being there. Only thoughts of Morg now stirred him to hatred. Only Morg's presence at the platform prevented him from deserting this place, to seek re-admittance there. They had taken Ela and Lidi back. Perhaps they would take him, also. He was, after all, one of the children. Lately, Gyre had almost ceased to enjoy the thought of himself as a hunter, and had sought to take refuge in his childhood. He was not, he told himself, responsible for any of the things which had happened. He was only a boy. He was here because his father had brought him. That was all. But then he would think about Morg, and the jealousy would come back, and he knew then why he was here, and why he could never return. And instead of hatred and defiance, he felt mostly a sadness, mixed up with his jealousy. He threw the empty skin on to the slush and looked downhill. Morg was coming out of the trees. Gyre gaped.

'Father!' he yelled.

Gawl poked his head through the doorway.

'Father! Morg is coming. He is down there.'

Gawl came out, spear in hand.

'Stay here. I will go to him,' he said, and he moved down the waterlogged snow, spear at the ready.

Morg carried no weapon. The thong at his waist had no knife. Gawl smiled with his mouth, thinly. Another few paces, and the boy would not escape his throw, even if he turned and ran. When a man's length was between them, they stopped. The first trees were a spear's throw away. Morg spoke.

'Put up your spear, Gawl. I come with words for you, from the chief.'

The spear remained where it was.

'From *your* chief,' snarled Gawl, 'not *mine*.'

'Words of peace,' said Morg, quietly. 'Put up your spear.'

Gawl's eyes narrowed.

'I want no words from you, nor from any of your people. You are a fool to come here, unarmed, for now you will die.'

The words were hissed, and the spear-arm went back, slowly. Morg pointed to the trees.

'In there is Modd. He has his bow, and he would gladly see you dead. Kill me, and you will die, also.'

Gawl peered into the dark of the trees. He could see nobody, but the spear came down until its point rested on the snow. The arrows of Modd do not miss.

'Say your words, and go,' he grated.

Morg told him of the chief's offer. As he listened, Gawl's mouth twisted in mockery, and his face reddened. Morg finished speaking. Gawl's voice was taut with suppressed anger as he replied, 'Why does the old fool send to *me* his offer? It is *I* who could offer terms to *him*: to *all* of you! *I* have the flint. You have none. *We* have full bellies. You have not. See!' And he pointed a shaking hand towards the carcasses on the slope. The women had stopped work, and were watching. They could not make out what was being said. Trond and Alpa were coming down the hill, slowly, and Gawl waved them back with a sweep of his arm. They stopped. He turned back to Morg.

'Meat. Skins. Flint. What do *we* need with your offer? And if the children pine for their mothers; what is that to me? They ran away. Now go. And when we meet again, it is *you* who will seek to hear *my* offer!'

Morg gestured towards the huts.

'Will you not ask your people?' he asked. 'It is important for them.'

Gawl glowered.

'*I* am leader here!' he raged. '*I* decide what my people will do!' The spear came up again. 'Go!'

Morg took two steps backwards. The women were coming down the slope. Trond and Alpa were moving again, also. Gyre remained by his father's hut. Morg shouted so that all could hear.

'You are free to return: all of you. Ask Gawl!'

He turned, and strode towards the trees. Gawl aimed his spear at the retreating back, and an arrow kicked up a spurt of snow between his feet. He lowered the weapon, glared into the trees, and turned on his heels.

He had to break through the semicircle of his people halfway up the slope.

'What did he mean?' said Trond. 'I want to go to my child!'

The others were muttering also. Only Jodi was silent. Gawl strode through, screaming at them to drown out their voices.

'It was nothing! Nothing! He came with an offer. They are fools. They will die. Get to your work!'

He ducked into his lodge. Jodi followed him. He was kneeling on a pile of skins, holding his head. His teeth were bared in a silent snarl, and he shook. The woman knelt beside him, and placed a hand on his shoulder. He took down his hands, and looked at her.

'Listen to them,' he whispered, desperately. 'Listen to their voices. I cannot hold them now. They will go back. Even Gyre will go back.'

Jodi spoke, softly.

'It is a trap. You must tell them that it is a trap.

Tell them that if they go back, they will be killed. The platform people want only the flint.'

Gawl shook his head, wearily.

'No. They speak the truth. They *will* take my people back. But *I* cannot go. I will die, alone.'

Jodi took him by both shoulders, and shook him.

'They believe you. You can make them believe you. If you tell them it is a trap, they will believe that, and stay. They are fools. You can sway them with your speaking. You have always done this. They admire your courage. Your hunting never fails. They will follow you for the sake of their bellies.'

Gawl sighed.

'They are dissatisfied. They talk of nothing else.'

'They have nothing else to think on,' the woman said. 'You must give them something.'

The tired leader looked into her eyes.

'What?'

Jodi leaned forward, earnestly, waving her arms for emphasis.

'Give them something to fight,' she rapped, 'so that they will stop fighting *you*. Make a plan, to attack the platform. Tell them of your plan. Tell them that if we do not attack *them*, then they will attack *us*. Say that their trap failed, because you saw their offer for what it was. Now they will attack, if we do not strike first. Tell them all this. And when you have captured the platform, you will have them for ever, for there is nowhere else for them to go.'

She sank back, watching him. He was silent a while, frowning. Then he said, 'If we attack the platform, we might die.'

Jodi shrugged.

'If they *return* to the platform, you *will* die. Seize your chance. You can be master still.'

The voices outside had dropped to a low muttering. Jodi helped her man to his feet, and pushed him softly towards the doorway.

'Go,' she whispered. 'Be angry. That is what they expect. Show no doubt; no weakness. That is what they are waiting for. Go.' He suppressed a shudder, and ducked into the sunlight.

Alpa and Trond loitered on the slope, looking back to where Gawl stood with Jodi. He was taking much time to say his farewells to her. Gyre stood nearby, so the two said nothing. Trond ground his spear haft into the soft turf, and leaned his weight on it. All three were heavily laden with weapons. Besides their spears, each carried a bow and many arrows. Their belts were hung about with axes and knives, so that the thongs were taut on their hips.

Presently Gawl, similarly laden, turned and began to move towards them. Jodi was coming down behind him. She was saying something to Gawl which the others could not hear. When they were near, Alpa said, 'Why does the woman come?'

Gawl did not reply, but walked on past his followers, and Jodi followed him. The others fell into line behind them, and they entered the trees.

'Women do not hunt,' said Alpa. 'Why does Jodi come with us?'

Gawl walked on silently. Jodi turned her head.

'It is a law of the platform people, that women do

not hunt,' she said. 'It is not *our* law. I can throw a spear. There will be danger. I will be needed.'

Alpa only grunted, dropping his eyes. Jodi walked on before him, and kept herself always between Gawl's back and the spears of his people.

A warm night had carried the snow away, and the earth beneath the trees was muddy. Mist hung faintly yellow, and a hazy sun glowed behind the boughs. The party moved swiftly, their bare feet making slapping and sucking noises in the mud. There was only this, and the sounds of the birds. Trond, bringing up the rear, gazed at the slight figure of Gyre ahead of him without really seeing. He was adrift on his thoughts. The platform people had tried to trap them: to lure them back to their deaths. They wanted the flint.

'And I would have gone back,' he mused, 'if Gawl had not seen the trap. He is wiser, perhaps, than I have thought.'

And he looked across the bobbing heads in front of him, to where Gawl was walking in a crouch, his spear thrust out before him; and a feeling of affection and trust glowed in him for his leader. 'He speaks sometimes in haste, but in danger, there is no better leader than Gawl,' he told himself.

Jodi was following her man very closely, so that Trond could only see him from time to time, and he turned his unseeing gaze on the boy's back and trudged on.

They were going around the south end of the lake, and the water was sometimes visible through the trees to the north. Gawl glanced at the sun. Midday. Half their journey was done. Soon, it would be time to leave the forest, and to slip into the swamp, where there was no chance of running into a hunting party from the platform, and where the thick, high reeds would mask their approach. The journey was shorter round the north end of the lake, but Gawl had chosen this way because the swamp was wider at this side, giving better cover. He was about to give the order to turn towards the lake, when he heard voices. He froze, holding up an arm to halt his followers. All strained to hear. The faint sounds came again, mixed up with birdsong. Gawl motioned for the others to come quietly round him.

'There is a hunting party,' he whispered. 'If we go now into the swamp, we could take the platform while the men are away. But they might return before our work was done, and catch us in the open. If we kill the hunting party here, then the platform is easily ours. This we will do.'

Jodi said, 'Where are they, and how far?'

Alpa pointed to the west.

'That way, and three stones' throws distant.'

Gawl held up his hand for silence.

'We will use our bows, so that we need not be too close to them. Prepare your weapons, and stay behind me. If Morg is with the party, I will bring him down myself.'

The group moved softly over the mud towards the voices. Another sound became audible; a rhythmic creaking, like an old, split tree in the wind. Gawl stopped, puzzled. His raised hand halted the party. They listened. The creaking came nearer. Voices were shouting. Trond's voice came, too loud.

'These are not the people.'

The men paled, and looked wide-eyed to their leader. Gawl looked dumbly back at them. There *were* no other people. This he knew. But voices were there in the forest. Voices he did not know. They stood, stricken. The sounds came nearer. Jodi whispered, urgently, 'Into the trees. They come near. We will see.' She turned, reached up to a low crotch, and hauled herself up into the tracery of limbs. The others watched her, but did not follow. Somewhere, a sapling splintered. Weight was coming, like an old bear, crunching bracken underfoot with ponderous indifference. Movement, there, between the trees. The men scattered, and flung themselves into the dead wetness of the bracken. Gyre burrowed, pulling the brittle fronds over himself until his hands scrabbled in the slimy rottenness of the root-clumps. He held his breath, to make the fronds stop trembling over him. His cheek lay along the spongy mould and its pungent reek was in his nostrils. His arms were extended beyond his head, and one hand gripped the bow. His arrow was gone. He dared not move to fit another. No use to fit another. The lost ones do not die with arrows. Voices, very near now. A trembling in the earth, and everywhere the rhythmic creaking, like swinging on a dead limb. Gyre kept his head down until he could bear it no longer. They were all about him. The ground moved, like a herd of buffalo running by. He raised his head.

The forest was filled with people. They came swarming between the trees. They called out to one another with strange words. Some of the men carried long, thin spears, and others had knives or clubs in their belts. There were women. Gyre's eyes widened as he looked at these women. Their faces were daubed with colours, and they wore strips of hide twisted into their hair, with sparkling things here and there upon them. One of the women had many amber beads hung about her neck. Her hair was pale. It was almost like the hair of Old Gart, but the woman was not old. There were more people than all of the cliff people and all of the platform people together. And in the middle of the swarm moved the thing that was making the creaking noise. Gyre caught his breath, and stared. The thing was like nothing he had ever seen. Men swarmed around it, lugging and pushing. A picture came to Gyre of the platform people, pushing the dugout across the boughs towards the water. It was not a dugout. A dugout moved only a little way at a time, when the men strained all together. A dugout jerked along, and made deep marks along the ground where it had passed. This thing moved without jerking. It did not stop with its nose jammed under boughs and mud. Its nose was not on the ground, but up, half a man's height from the ground. It was like . . . Gyre frowned with the effort of concentration. It was like a big dugout; but no tree was thick enough to make a dugout so wide. It was wide, and long, and not round. Not round like a tree. And it moved along with its nose up, smoothly. And something beside it bigger than the moon, turning over, and over, and over . . .

A man shouted, pointing. The creaking thing stopped. The man who shouted ran forward and bent swiftly.

He straightened, and Gyre's arrow was in his hand. Gyre gasped, and ducked his head. Voices jabbered, excitedly. The boy waited, tense; then slowly raised his head. The people were in a tight huddle around the dugout-thing. The men held their spears at the ready, and looked all around. Gyre saw that they were afraid. Behind them, the women, some holding children. The men were looking all around, and jabbering to one another with strange, fast words. Then one of them saw Jodi. He was pointing to her tree. Gyre could see her, flattened against the trunk, up among the naked branches. He felt quickly for an arrow, and fitted it to his bow. The bracken crackled when he moved, but the other people were making too much noise to hear. Two men were moving towards Jodi's tree. They were still too far away to throw their spears. To do this, they would have to pass closer to Gyre. He tautened his bowstring, waiting. Jodi was crabbing around her tree, trying to keep the trunk between herself and the men. They were still beyond a spear's throw. Gyre started, as Gawl's strident yell burst through the forest: 'Jodi! Jump, Jodi; run, before they throw!'

Gawl was up, running for her tree. The men around the dugout-thing whirled, pointing their spears towards him; Gyre came to his knees, aiming. The two men had stopped. They pointed their weapons at Jodi.

'They are still beyond throw,' he muttered.

Jodi ran out, balancing, along a limb, preparing to leap.

There came a sharp sound, like an axe striking a stone, and she fell out of the tree. Gawl howled horribly, and swerved towards the two men, his spear raised. Another sharp crack, and the enraged hunter spun round and dropped into the bracken. Gyre shot his arrow, and one of the men pitched forward, the shaft rigid between his shoulders. The other man turned, hurled his spear at Gyre, and ran towards the others. The spear took the boy in the chest and he fell. In the dark bracken, Gyre rolled over, and found himself unhurt. The spear lay beside him. It was only a shaft, blunt and gleaming. He came to his feet and ran, crouching. There were shouts, and the sharp sound came again, twice, but Gyre ran on. Away to one side of him he could see Trond, jinking away through the trees. Vaguely, he wondered whether Alpa had escaped, also. Gawl had fallen; Jodi had died. And the spears that killed them had remained in the hands of their killers. This he had seen, clearly. There was no mistake. Terror swept over him, and he ran on, pounding his bare feet into the mud until the sounds behind him faded and ceased.

The sun's rim was on the lake when Gawl came out of the trees. Trond shouted to Gyre, and all the cliff people came to stand by the wall, watching him come up the slope. He came slowly, and one arm hung at his side. There was blood. When he saw the wall, Gawl stopped. A line of boughs, stones and bushes, piled almost man high, curved across the slope. The two ends of the wall were at the cliff edge. The settlement was cut off from the lower slopes and from the forest.

His people were watching him across the wall. He came on. When Gawl was near, Gyre pushed aside some bushes and a trunk, and went through the gap to his father.

'We saw you fall, Father,' he said. 'We thought you dead.'

Gawl gazed at the boy blankly.

'Jodi is dead,' he mumbled.

They came in through the gap. Alpa and Trond pulled the trunk back, and piled up the bushes again. Gawl shambled towards the huts. Gyre walked beside him.

'Make a fire,' muttered Gawl. 'It is cold here.'

Gyre took his father's arm, guiding him towards his own lodge.

'We cannot make fire,' he said. 'The smoke would bring the other people.'

At the doorway, Gawl stopped. Alpa was near the wall, with his spear. The others were coming up the slope. Trond said, 'The other people will come. We made the wall. We thought you dead.'

Gawl looked at him without replying.

'Gyre said make a wall,' continued Trond. 'Gyre said make no fire. But we do not know what to do, without a fire. How can we have no fire, in the night when there are the lost ones? How can we hunt, in the forest, when there are the other people?'

He broke off, expectantly.

Gawl looked at the desperate faces of his people, and said nothing.

Reda cried, 'We should have returned to the platform. Now we cannot. Now we will die . . .' Hila stopped her with a sharp glance. She came close to Gawl.

'I will take care of little Pab,' she said gently, 'and tend your wound. Only tell us what we are to do.'

Gawl stared at her, without seeing. Then he said, 'What does Gyre say that we are to do?'

10

Daf threw down the hares and went quickly to the chief's hut. Morg looked up from his pot of resin and saw the frown on his face. The boy followed with his eyes, as his father ducked into the low entrance. A good hunt: but something else. Something had worried Daf. Something to do with the cliff people? Morg got to his feet, and walked slowly across the platform. A murmuring came from the dimness within, but the boy could not make out the words. He stood impatiently, shuffling his feet on the worn boughs, until his father emerged. The frown was still there.

'Ah, Morg,' he grunted. 'There is a bad thing: there is something that we do not understand.'

He came close, laying an arm across the shoulders of his son, and they moved away together towards the landing-stage.

'In the forest, I have found Jodi. She is dead. She has a wound, as from an arrow, but there is no arrow. There are broken sticks, and the grasses are flat. There are tracks. This is near to us: the tracks show that all the cliff men came to this place, one day past.' He paused.

Morg said, 'Jodi, also? Jodi came with the men?'

Daf nodded slowly, and his frown deepened.

'There are other tracks. Very many. They are strange; tracks of men with no toes.'

'Men!' cried Morg. 'Tracks of men? But there are no men; no men but the people.'

Daf spoke, sharply.

'There are tracks of things that walk upon two legs. This I have seen. The lost ones make no tracks. This I know. Men have toes: their tracks, also, have toes. These tracks have no toes. Men with no toes were in the forest. The cliff people saw: they ran away. Jodi is dead.'

He shrugged. There were no more words. They stood, gazing out across the water. There was no smoke from the cliff.

The hump stirred, so that the coloured thing slid down one side of it, and there was a man underneath. A startled bird shrieked and whirred away. The man stood up, slowly, knuckling his eyes. He yawned, noisily. The other coloured humps began to move, and soon the place under the trees was filled with people. The coloured things lay like crumpled skins on the ground. The first man bent, and lifted up his coloured skin-thing. He put it around his shoulders, and twisted a thong, so that it stayed on him like a robe. A child ran by, chased by another, squealing. People were moving around, putting on their skin-things, talking rapidly, like jays. The two children returned, carrying bark and twigs. They made a pile and a woman bent over it. She clicked something, sharply, and a wisp of smoke appeared, thickening. Another woman brought a pot, and tilted it over the small flame. Something spilled out, and the fire flared suddenly, crackling.

The first man walked slowly between the trees. He came to the place where the bundles were piled. A man squatted there with a spear that shone with the early sun. He was tired from his watch, and yawned a greeting. The two men exchanged words for a while; then the guard walked off towards the fire. The first man squatted down on a bundle, and laid the spear across his knees. After a while, a child came with food for him, and he ate slowly, turning his head all the while to look into the forest. The others made a many-coloured circle round the fire, and ate. Their chatter came to him on the faint wind. He finished his food, and wiped his beard with the back of his hand. All the time, he was watching the forest. His head turned slowly, and his eyes were screwed up. Suddenly, he uttered a sharp sound, and came to his feet. Away to the north, a thin column of smoke was visible between the budding tops. The man called towards the others, pointing. The people stood up to see, and excited voices echoed through the forest. A man began shouting, and the others gathered round him. He spoke quickly, gesticulating with his arms as he did so. His robe was red like the sun. Everybody listened to him. After a while, he stopped shouting, and came towards the bundles. All the others followed him. The first man crouched by one bundle, tugging at the thong around it. Spears spilled out, rattling. The men came and picked up spears, smiling and calling to one another like men at the end of a good hunt. The women watched, and smiled also. Children scampered about, lunging at one another with invisible weapons, and uttering cries of feigned pain. The first man gazed raptly towards the distant smoke. His mouth smiled, but the glint of malice made a hardness in his eyes.

The sun came up behind the trees so that it became hard to look towards the forest. Alpa rubbed his aching eyes and turned them towards the cluster of huts on the slope. The two women crouched by the dead ashpile, preparing food. Without fire, they could not cook, but habit caused them to come to the place to pound their mess of raw roots and red meat. Gyre came out of Gawl's hut, stretched, and walked towards the women. Alpa yawned. His face felt stiff. It had been a long, cold night; he had stood, tense with strain, and every sound from the blackness had caused him to start up, spear at the ready. There had been no fire, to keep the lost ones away, and if there had been fire, it would have been of little comfort to him: it was not the lost ones those anxious eyes had sought through the night. And when dawn rinsed away the shadows, so that the forest came back, even then his unease remained. The men of yesterday whose spears kill without being thrown, did not melt with the night into the west. He turned back wearily towards the trees.

Trond emerged from his shelter, yawning. He had slept brokenly and his fleeting dreams had been haunted with strange horrors. His woman looked up from the cooking-pot, beckoning. He shuffled over to the fire-place.

'Come, eat the food,' said Hila, 'and take some down to Alpa. It is poor food; we can make it no better, without the fire.'

Trond squatted, thrusting one hand into the pot, and scooping up a fistful of the cold, sticky mixture. He put the hand to his mouth, and chewed, looking over his knuckles at Gyre.

'Will Gawl come out today?' he asked, dully.

The boy lowered his eyes, and mumbled, 'I think not. I think Gawl will never come out again.'

A small furry bundle on the ground began to whine, and Reda picked it up. The face of little Pab was screwed up, reddening, and he kicked inside his cocoon. Reda rocked him.

'Why do you say this?' she said, looking at Gyre.

The boy shrugged.

'He has not eaten. He does not sleep. He does not speak. I think that he will go to the lost ones soon.'

Trond swallowed food and said, 'He must come out. We do not know what to do.'

Gyre shrugged again.

'We will stay here, and make no fire. Soon, the other men will go away and we will have fire again. Perhaps they are gone away now.'

Hila grunted, 'And perhaps they are not.'

A new thought came to Trond. 'Soon, the platform people will go to the hills. If the new people are gone, shall we also go to the hills?' His anxious eyes scanned Gyre's face.

'I do not know,' said Gyre, slowly. 'It is difficult.

Now there are men in the forest. They are not our friends.'

His young brow was puckered into a scowl with his effort to think. He saw in his mind the straggle of his people bent under their loads, moving slowly towards the teeming hills; and himself, and the other children, running through the trees, calling and laughing because it was the beginning of a time of plenty: because in the daytime, in the awakening forest, nothing existed which could hurt them. And now . . . He saw again the new people with their creaking thing. Pushing and jabbering. The skins they wore had many colours. There was a woman with pale hair and glittering things twisted into it. And the spears that shone: that killed and stayed in the hands of the men.

'It is – different, now,' he said. 'I think that we will stay here. There will be danger in the forest.'

'We will need to *hunt* in the forest,' said Trond, 'and we cannot live for ever without a fire.'

He stood up, scooping a double handful of food for Alpa.

'Gawl must come out. He will know what to do.' He turned, and went down the slope. Gyre watched him, blankly. Gawl would not come out. Whatever they were to do, it would have to be done without Gawl. Without the leader. The two women were watching him. Reda, rocking Pab on her shoulder, said, 'Somebody must decide. There should be a chief.'

Gyre scowled, and lowered his eyes. Why did they stare at *him?* He was a child. They were *all* older than he was. Hila said: 'Gawl spoke. He said. "What does

Gyre say that we are to do?"' She paused. Gyre gazed down the slope, hugging his knees. 'What does Gyre say that we are to do?' she repeated.

Gyre heard, but made no reply. Down at the wall, Alpa and Trond were talking. He could see their lips moving, and the gestures of their arms. The women saw the direction of his gaze. Hila spoke.

'Trond and Alpa are men. They are not leaders of men. They hear, and follow. Now they hear nothing.'

Gyre bit his lip. It is a fine thing to be the son of a chief. To be respected by the people, because one day you will lead and they will follow. Because one day you will carry the burden your father carries. And their respect makes you feel like a chief, and you are happy, because you have the respect, and your father has the burden. Dread washed through the boy. He could not take the burden. Not yet. It was unfair. Gawl was still young. The burden was Gawl's. He raised his eyes to the eyes of the women and there was a plea in them. The women looked into the eyes of their leader, and saw a child.

'Gyre!' A shout from Alpa. 'Gyre! See.'

The distant figure was pointing back up the slope, towards the cliff top. The three looked where he was pointing. Two thin stains slanted up the sky. One was from the platform. The other pointed towards the southern end of the lake. Gyre ran to the cliff top, followed by Hila and Reda. They stood, looking out over the placid water. The two men came up, panting.

'They are still nearby,' gasped Trond, 'and they will see the smoke from the platform.'

Hila looked at him, wildly.

'Ela!' she cried. 'Ela is there. She will die.'

'And Lidi,' breathed Alpa.

The four turned to Gyre.

'What must we do?' demanded Reda, wild-eyed. 'Our children will die.' Gyre, open-mouthed, looked at them with blank eyes. He shook his head slowly, in a dazed way. Then he turned, and ran down the slope to his father's hut. Gawl lay as before, huddled in his pile of skins. Gyre knelt beside him, and tugged desperately at his crumpled robe.

'Father!' he cried. 'There is smoke from the platform.'

Gawl rolled over, and gazed vacantly at his son. He said nothing. Gawl's blank expression dissolved slowly into a frown, and his eyes focused on the boy's face. Hope surged through. Gawl was going to speak. Gawl would tell them what to do. The lips moved, faintly, and the old fire burned in his eyes. Gyre bent close to hear.

'The platform people will die,' he croaked, 'and we shall be lords of the forest.'

Modd grunted, and shifted his weight on to the other foot. He leaned on his spear haft, and scanned the sloping ground once again. At the top of the bank, on dry ground, the forest crowded in, pushing a scattering of dwarf birches over the brink, so that they grew stuntedly on the slope, almost down to where the platform began. Here, marsh plants put up fresh shoots and the black raft had a fringe of green. Reed clumps grew along the slope, becoming small higher up; dying out where the birches grew. Many of the trees here were barkless and dying; Modd shuddered, remembering the time of famine.

The sun was warm on his back. It hung dimly glowing over the misty lake, and threw long shadows of the huts towards him. He glanced to his right. Morg was there, squatting at the foot of his spear haft, the point far above his head. He saw Modd looking, and raised an arm in greeting. Modd returned the salute, and yawned. Spring. Soon, they ought to be leaving the platform for the hills. The hills, teeming with tender young meat and clothed in succulent shoots. A time of plenty, when the hunting was easy, and the children became fat to face a far-off winter.

But this time it was different. Now there were the cliff people; now there were men without toes, also. Today, there had been a fire in the forest; it showed where the toeless ones were. Old Gart had made them put out their own fire; the toeless ones had killed Jodi. They might follow the smoke, and kill again here. Modd and Morg guarded the platform. Today, Mow and Lidi did not gather shoots, or splash in the shallows. Cyl's antler pick remained propped against Daf's hut wall. There would be no roots dug out today. The women stayed close to their huts, and the children stayed close to the women. In the chief's hut, the two old men talked in low voices, their white heads nodding together. Near the landing, Daf sat with a pile of hafts, sharpening them at one end. The whole platform lay as though in waiting.

The sun rose higher over the water, and the mist

dispersed. The women busied themselves with skins, since there was no fire to cook with.

Morg, still squatting, began to drowse. He watched, with half-closed eyes, a bird gathering dry reeds for its nest. It would come, skimming down the slope, to alight at the platform's rim. There it would peck about, until it found a loose stalk. This it would drag clear of the tangle, working with sudden, jerky movements of its head, and shrilling to itself from time to time. Having freed the brittle stem, it would take a grip and launch itself into the air, flying clumsily up the bank with the reed trailing on the ground, to vanish over the rim into the forest. Morg smiled faintly. A nest. Soon there would be eggs. Tomorrow he would follow the bird to find where the nest was, and when the eggs came, he would take them, and bring them to Ela, so that she would remember how he had brought eggs to her when she was small.

The bird was here again, among the tangle of last summer's reeds. Tomorrow, when the new people were gone . . . The bird bobbed erect, head tilted, listening. Something of the acute tension in the tiny body communicated itself to Morg, and he held his breath, ears straining. A moment of total stillness, then the bird went, a dry whirring blur across the slope. Morg came to his feet, a sharp call on his lips. Modd shot a glance at the boy, and faced the slope, spear at the ready. As yet, there was nothing to hear.

'If only I had the ears of that bird,' thought Morg.

He felt fear; like when the angry, wounded bear came at him on that faraway slope. He was a man. Looking down at his scarred legs, he sucked in air, and gripped his spear more tightly, to keep it from trembling.

Modd called to the others, without turning his head. Daf came, carrying an armful of sharpened hafts.

'What is it?' he asked, tensely. 'What do you see?'

'I see nothing,' said Modd. 'But Morg hears . . .'

A flock of birds exploded shrieking from the trees, whirring over the platform and out across the lake. Daf dropped his burden, and the three men stared keenly into the tree-line. Faint, intermittent rustlings. A twig snapping. All along the bank top.

'Spread out!' hissed Modd, waving Daf away.

Daf crabbed along the rim, until he stood midway between Modd and Morg. He darted glances to either side. There was too much space between them.

Old Gart came up, and the chief.

'They come,' said Daf, tersely. 'They are in the trees. There is too much space between us. They are many.'

'There will be less space now.'

As he spoke, the old chief took up a position between Daf and Morg. Old Gart hobbled to the gap between Daf and Modd. He stood twistedly, a spear gripped in his claw-like hands. Modd called, 'You cannot stand with us, old man. You will die.' Old Gart spat, noisily, and croaked, 'Close your mouth, and use your ears, or we shall all die.'

The sounds were clearer now, and grasses twitched here and there on the rim of the bank.

'They lie in the grass, watching us,' called the chief.

Modd bent, putting down his spear, and unslung his

bow. He fitted an arrow, and watched closely. Almost directly above him, a frond bobbed, jerkily. Behind the fringe of stems, something moved, half-masked. Modd aimed, and shot at the place. There came a thud, and a cry. The grasses parted, and a man rose on his knees, clutching at the shaft that protruded from his shoulder. Hands grabbed at him, and he was dragged back out of sight. Modd fitted another arrow. He was smiling.

Beside him, Old Gart hissed, 'Smile when they are *all* hit; they are still far more than we.'

'Beware!' cried the chief. 'They come.'

They rose as if they were growing out of the ground; a line of men whose coloured robes glowed with the sun, and their spears flashed, and they came down the slope running. Their cries were harsh, their expressions exultant.

At the end of the line, Morg marked his man, and waited. The man hurtled down towards him, yelling. Something swished past Morg's ear, and then the man leapt off the slope towards the platform. The spear took him in the air, and he screamed, doubled up, and crashed on to the boughs at the boy's feet. His hair was red.

'Like a fox,' thought Morg, as he jerked his spear free.

Another man was launching himself at the platform. Morg swung his spear like a club. The haft smashed into the contorted face, and blood welled from the spattered nose. Turning the weapon, Morg thrust the point at his staggering adversary. The man collapsed, half on the platform. A third man checked his rush halfway down the slope, raising his spear. A click, and Morg cried out as pain seared his arm. The man turned and scrambled back up the bank. At the rim he jerked erect and toppled backwards into a clump of dwarf birches. Morg glanced along the curve of the platform's edge. At the far end, Modd raised an arm to him, grinning, and reloaded his bow.

The new people were running back up the bank and into the trees. Four lay motionless near the platform, and two others lay on the slope. All the defenders were still standing, and Morg turned his attention to his arm. It was bloody from a gash that ran from wrist to elbow. He knelt quickly, scooping up a handful of mud from between the reed clumps, and pressing this on to the wound. It stung, and he winced. When the mud dried, the bleeding would stop. The chief called to him.

'You are hurt. Can you hold your place?'

Morg saw in his mind the numbers of their enemies.

'I can hold my place,' he called back.

The men he had killed lay at his feet. He looked at them curiously. The nearer one wore a robe of a yellow colour. His hair was pale, and his feet had something fastened on to them with thongs. Morg touched one of the things. It was flat and hard and thick. Suddenly he understood the toeless tracks. He called to Daf.

'They have toes as we have. They fasten hooves on their feet with thongs!'

Daf nodded, and bent to a body that lay close to him. Modd was holding one of the shining spears; turning it in his hands.

'This spear has no point!' he cried, holding it up for the others to see.

Morg picked up a spear that lay nearby. There was no point on it, either. It felt cold. He could see his likeness in it, like looking into a pool. It was hollow at one end, like a reed. He lifted it to his nose. It smelled sharp, like the taste of blood. He frowned. On the slope, the spears had had points on them. Now they had not. He saw in his mind Modd shooting an arrow. Spears that shoot arrows. He dropped the weapon. The second body lay on its back. He prodded it with his foot, rolling it over. On the back, fastened there with a strip of hide, was a pouch: a quiver, like Modd's. He knelt, and withdrew a short, heavy shaft. It was cold like the spear, and gleaming. It had no feathers. There was a hole through the shaft where the feathers should be. The other end was sharpened. There was no head; it was all of one substance. Morg touched the point to the wounded place on his arm and nodded to himself. A shadow fell across him, and he started up. Old Gart looked down at him. There was a strange expression on his crumpled face.

'Put down the weapon, and hold your place,' he croaked, softly.

Morg hesitated, gazing at the smooth shaft with wonder.

'What is it, old man?' he asked. 'What is it made from? How does it fly?'

Old Gart shook his head, slowly.

'Do not seek to know,' he rattled. 'It is a thing of the lost ones.'

'But these are *men*!' cried Morg. 'Men use this weapon. How can it be a thing of the lost ones?'

Old Gart turned away, wearily.

'I hear them returning. Stand in your place,' he said.

They came, swarming out of the trees, over the lip, and down the slope. This time they walked, and when they were a spear's throw from the platform, they stopped. There was no screeching. They came silently, and stood, watching. The defenders stared back. Morg drew back his arm to cast.

'No!' cried Old Gart. 'They are beyond throw. Wait.'

A man appeared on the bank above the others. His robe was red like the sun. He pointed to the chief, and then to a point immediately below himself. He said something, sharply. The chief looked at Old Gart.

'He asks me to approach him.'

Old Gart shook his white head.

'Do not go to him,' he said.

'They are many,' said the chief, quietly. 'My people will die.' The man pointed again, and spoke more sharply in his strange tongue. 'I will go,' said the chief, and stepped off the platform. The others watched as he went slowly up the slope. The women came from behind their huts, clutching the children's hands in their own. Every eye was on the tall frail figure, with its robe of black fur, as it ascended with dignity towards Red-robe. Tilde sobbed softly, and Ela circled her waist with one arm, holding her close.

The new men moved to let the chief pass between them, and, close below Red-robe, he stopped. Red-robe glared down at the old man haughtily. He began to speak, rapidly, gesticulating with his arms, first towards the little knot of people below on the platform, then towards a place far away in the east. The chief shook his head, and pointed west. Red-robe shouted at him, and pointed east again, across the lake. The chief shook his head, silently. Red-robe said something to his people. One of the men came up the slope with his spear. He stood near the chief, and pointed the spear. Red-robe pointed east once more, and spoke with a hiss. Modd raised his bow, but Old Gart motioned to him to lower it. Everybody waited. The old chief raised himself to his full height, and stared up at Red-robe. Then, emphatically, he shook his head again. A sharp word from Red-robe, and the man nearby raised his spear. There was a sharp click, and the old chief staggered, a thin shaft gleaming in his side. As he sank to his knees, the other men pointed their spears at the platform. Old Gart cried, 'Down! Fall down!'

A volley of clicks, and a cry from Tilde. Huddled on the boughs, Morg saw her jerking with pain, and Ela, trying to drag her away to the shelter of a hut. Old Gart was shouting again, brokenly.

'Up! Run up the slope to them, quickly!'

Modd, Daf and Morg flung themselves forward. On the slope, the new men were fumbling with their spears, reloading. Modd's bow twanged, and one man crumpled and rolled down the bank. Daf, higher than Morg, hurled his spear, and another man toppled backwards and lay twitching. The others, half-loaded, turned to scramble away. Red-robe whirled, and ran for the trees. Morg, panting, threw his spear into the retreating throng, but no man fell. At the rim, Daf raised his hand to stop his companions.

'No further. Do not follow them into the trees.'

Dimly, Morg realised that his father was probably now chief.

The new men melted away into the forest, and the three hunters turned to the slope. The old chief lay where he had fallen. Modd bent over him, briefly: then he took the black robe from the crumpled form and handed it to Daf. The three men went wearily down to the platform.

'Pull away the boughs, and pile them up on the new edge.' Old Gart's voice crackled, and he wheezed with the effort of his speaking. The three men bent to their task; pulling up the blackened boughs at the platform's edge, and throwing them in a heap behind them, so that a strip of marsh appeared between the edge and the slope. 'Keep going. It must be wider.'

Morg, straining at a slimy branch, gasped, 'Perhaps they are gone. We have killed many of them.'

'There are many more,' croaked Old Gart. 'They will not go.'

'Why do they want to kill us?' grunted Modd. 'There is food enough for all.'

'Because we live, and are not of their people,' said Gart.

The strip of black ooze grew wider. When it was too wide for a man to leap over, Old Gart said that it was enough. They piled up the limbs they had taken out, so that there was a wall along the new edge. Morg surveyed the work.

‘Now they cannot hit us from the slope, and they cannot cross the marsh. They will go away.’

‘They will not go away, until all their hunters are dead,’ said Gart.

‘They are very many,’ Morg replied, looking anxiously at the old man. ‘We will have no weapons left to kill them all.’

Gart nodded slowly.

‘I know,’ he said.

At the landing, Ela, Morg’s mother, and the woman of Modd were putting things into the dugout. Cooking-pots, lamps, knives, scrapers and needles lay in the bottom of the craft, and Tilde, the wound in her thigh bound with mud and leaves, sat near the blunt prow, on a pile of skins. Mow and Lidi stood nearby.

‘Stay near to the dugout,’ Daf told his woman. ‘If I call to you to go, then take the children and go at once. There is room in the dugout for three women, and Mow and Lidi. Ela and Cyl must be in the water, holding on to the dugout, one at each side. Paddle to the cliff. Tell the cliff people what has happened here. Tell them to take their things and go away from the lake. Make no fire for many days.’

He stood for a moment, watching the women’s preparations. They worked quickly, with concentration, so as to avoid thinking about what was about to happen to the men.

A shout from Morg made him turn. Following the direction of his son’s pointing hand, he was in time to see Red-cloak ducking back from the bank top and making for the trees. Dim figures flitted in the edge of the forest.

'They are coming again,' croaked Old Gart. 'Down behind the wall, all of you, where I have put the stakes.'

The old man had divided the sharpened hafts into four piles, and laid them spaced out behind the wall of boughs. Daf walked rapidly over, and crouched beside one of the piles. The four men gazed over the wall, and waited.

Presently, sounds began to echo in the trees. There were shouts, and a repeated thudding. It seemed to come from some distance away. The four men glanced at one another. Daf could see the puzzlement in the faces of Morg and Modd, but Old Gart's expression seemed more knowing in some way: as though he had been expecting something which was now happening. The grey head nodded slowly to itself, and Daf heard the low hum of self-confirmation.

'What is it, old man?' he called, gruffly. 'What are they doing?'

A heavy crash sounded out, and then another.

'They cut down trees,' he said, answering his own question.

'But why?' said Modd. 'What will they do with trees?'

Morg, at the end of the line, called, 'Perhaps they will cross the swamp on them. Eh, old man?' he added, as no response came from Gart.

The old man shook his head.

'I think not,' he rattled.

The three men waited for him to go on but he said no more; only crouched there crookedly, staring into the trees. Morg was puzzled. Gart seemed almost to know about these people; as though he knew their ways. His answers were misty, but they seemed to come from knowing.

'Old man,' he called, 'did you know, before, that there were these people?'

Gart stared at the forest, and said nothing.

Modd joined in.

'You are not afraid. Their ways are strange, but you do not fear them.'

Old Gart grunted, without turning his head.

'I am afraid. I fear them more than you.'

'Listen!' Daf's urgent voice cut across their talk.

The old sounds had stopped. Now there was a low rumbling, and a rhythmic creaking sound, which grew louder. Now and then there was a noise like a wounded elk running into a tree, and then the men could be heard, grunting and shouting.

The four hunters crouched tense behind their wall. Something was in the forest edge. There was movement. Something huge, there in the shadows. The sun was beginning to slide down the sky over the black trees, and it was not easy to see. But the thing was coming out, and the new people with it. They crowded around it, pulling and pushing. It was higher than two men, and moved very slowly. Morg screwed up his eyes, and tried to stop his trembling. It was made with trees. The trees were fastened together, so that some of them stood up on others that lay down, on the ground. The new men had the thing tied with long ropes, which they pulled. And the trees on the ground rolled over slowly, and the thing rumbled forward. Morg gasped. It came to him that the new men had made this thing, in the forest, in so small a time. Awe seized him as he looked at them. What could they not do?

'What is this, Gart?' cried Daf.

Gart hissed, 'Go to the dugout. Bring water-skins.' He spoke urgently, waving his crooked arms in agitation. 'Quickly, quickly!'

Daf ran, crouching across the platform. The ancient hunter motioned to Morg and Modd to come to him.

'Fill the skins,' he wheezed. 'Keep them by you. They will be needed.' Morg started to speak. 'Enough! Do not question. There is no time.' He pointed.

They were doing something to the tree-thing. They pulled down one of the standing trees with a rope. It came down slowly. It was like a great paddle, this tree; a huge flat blade was on the end of it. Like a paddle for a dugout, but bigger than two dugouts. A man reached up to the paddle, and pushed a great armful of twigs and grasses on to it. The paddle was turned up at the edges like a cooking-pot, so that the twigs and grasses stayed there without falling off. Another man brought a pot. He reached up and poured water on to the bundle. Red-robe was standing at the rim of the slope, looking down at the hunters. He was smiling with his mouth.

Old Gart said, 'Morg. Tell the women to go, with the dugout. Tell them to go *now*.' Morg hesitated.

'Go!' cried Gart.

The boy ran, passing his father coming from the landing with skins.

'The women go!' he called as they passed.

He held the weeping Ela in his arms, as the dugout was pushed clear. The craft was overloaded, and low in the water. Cyl held on to it with one hand, treading water.

'You must go, Ela,' he told her softly. 'Gart knows these people. He knows that the tree-thing is bad. You must go now,' he repeated. He pushed her gently towards the craft, but she clung to him. Over her shoulder, Morg could see his mother, sitting dumbly among the bundles, her face streaked with tears.

'Take care of my mother,' he whispered.

Ela nodded, mechanically.

'Yes,' she choked. 'Yes.'

She clambered into the swaying dugout. Somewhere behind them, there was a swishing sound, and Morg whirled. A ball of fire arced across the sky, turning slowly, over and over. Cries of terror broke from the women. Lidi screamed.

'Go!' shrieked Morg, and pushed the dugout desperately outwards.

The fireball came over the wall, hit the platform, bounced, and rolled into the skeleton of an empy hut which exploded into flames. Morg shot a last glance at the wallowing dugout and ran towards the wall.

Daf was crouching near the flames, holding a teeming water-skin over the blaze. Steam hissed malevolently among the glowing boughs. Gart and Modd crouched at the wall, watching the slope. The new men stood round the tree-thing, looking down at the defenders. No man came down the bank. Red-robe was shouting, and a new bundle was on the paddle. Modd drew back his bow, and loosed an arrow. A man by the paddle cried out and fell, but another man reached up, and the bundle burst into flame.

The paddle sprang upright, and another ball came over, shedding burning fragments, and trailing a thin smoke bow. It crashed on to the boughs and split apart. Pieces of burning material spun in all directions, and here and there, the platform caught fire.

'Water!' screeched Gart, and he ran twistedly, dragging a full skin. Morg grabbed another, and poured it on to a blazing part. A shout on the slope, and a shower of bright shafts fell among the smoke. Morg dropped his skin, and dived for the wall. Modd shot an arrow in reply, which narrowly missed Red-robe. He moved to stand behind the tree-thing. The four hunters crouched close to their barrier of boughs. Behind them the platform smouldered in places, and little flames ran here and there along strips of dry bark. The men on the slope stood with weapons raised, so that the defenders could do nothing to quench the fire.

Morg peered over the barrier. His eyes stung with the smoke, and the hate burned in him.

'We are helpless,' he told himself bitterly. 'We cannot overcome these men. They need only stand there, and we must cower here and burn.' He called to his father.

'We can only die here. We might as well charge the slope, and die like hunters.'

Daf shook his head, stubbornly.

'No. The sun is low. When darkness comes, we will slip away through the reed beds.'

Modd flexed his bow, and grunted.

'When darkness comes, we will be dead; is that not so, old man?'

Gart shrugged.

the blood. But nothing could take away the butchery, or even cover it over. It was a part of him now. Of them all.

Something gleamed at his feet. He stooped, picking up the slim, cold shaft. Strange people, with strange things. He examined the shaft. What was it made from? How was it fired? It was necessary to know. To understand.

'If there are people with such weapons, then we must have them, also. We must not be weak, any more,' he said, half aloud.

A sound on the slope made him start. He tensed, shaft gripped tight. Three figures were coming down, kicking up the ashes. All carried spears. Morg backed, slowly. The nearest figure raised its arm in greeting, and called out. It was Gyre, blackened with ash and smoke. And behind him came Trond and Alpa, grinning. Their teeth gleamed in their black faces.

Morg ran to the edge, holding out an arm to the wading Gyre, pulling him on to the platform. The boy grinned up at him.

'A good fire,' he said. 'You saw the fire? We *made* the fire.' He laughed, pointing to his companions, who were pulling their legs out of the mud. 'I took them into the reed beds, and we made bundles, like the new people. When they came down to the platform, we laid our bundles in the grass, and fired them. All along the top.'

Morg looked at the smaller boy incredulously.

'*You* led them? Then where is Gawl?'

'Gawl is dead.'

Modd was coming along the platform. Gyre glanced

towards the big warrior, apprehensively. He still carried the great axe.

'Will we be welcome here?' he asked uncertainly.

Morg laughed.

'After such a fire, you need not ask,' he said. 'You saved us all.'

'The wind was right,' said Gyre, quietly.

'Modd has gone to the cliff. He will bring the women tomorrow, and the children.' Old Gart nodded. 'It is well.'

The people sat close together, and the firelight danced in their eyes.

'It will be good, when we are all together,' ventured Alpa.

'It will be good,' sighed Morg. 'There will be much to say.'

'There will be much to do, also,' said Gyre. 'The platform is half gone.'

Daf shook his head.

'Tomorrow, we go to the hills. This has been a good place. We shall not be here again. It is – different, now.'

'How, different?' asked Trond.

'From now on,' said Old Gart, sadly, 'the people will live on a hill. It will be their hill, and no other man will climb it.'

He paused, looking slowly round at the people. Only he knew all that they had lost.

'We must not be weak, any more,' he said.

11

The fire felt good, and Lidi, cheek pressed hard into her mother's robe, held out her hands to the warmth. An owl ghosted down into the valley and its lonely call echoed away through the hills. The people huddled close, making a tight circle around the flames, and a great cold moon hung in the blackness above them. Trond spoke softly, across the flames.

'Old man. Tell us a story.'

The talking stopped, and Old Gart looked around at the expectant faces.

'Which story?' he croaked, after a while.

'The story of long ago. The tale your father told to you,' said Trond, and murmurs of approval told him that the people agreed with his choice.

The old man pulled his robe closely about him, and settled himself more comfortably in his place. The people waited patiently. It was their favourite tale, and anticipation was a part of the pleasure.

A wolf howled, far away. Gart waited, until the echo shivered away to silence; then he began:

'Long, long ago, before the great beast roamed the

forest, and before the forest grew, the world had more people than the hills have stalks of grass.

'These people were mighty; their villages were long, and their shelters were made from the rocks. And the people cut the rocks, and shaped them, and raised them one upon another; and their shelters were high, and so strong that the greatest wind could blow, and they would not fall.

'And these people took the sand, and turned it into rock for their shelters. And they made the great flying things, and the great water things, and the lamps that never die; and they made the things that talk.

'And these people did not hunt. They made roots to grow for them; and the beasts stayed near to the people, and the people fed them and ate them.'

Old Gart paused, to rest his throat, and the people sighed, for the hundredth time, to think of such a time; if only it were not just a tale.

'These people flew like the birds in the sky,' the old man continued, 'and swam like the fish below the water; and many and wonderful were the things that they could do; but these people were unwise. They fought among themselves.'

Here, the people round the fire looked covertly at one another, and there was discomfort, and shuffling.

'This story, also, is different now,' thought Morg.

'And their fighting was the more terrible, because of the wonderful things they could do. And there came a dreadful time: a time of thunder and flames in the sky. And when it stopped, there was a great stillness. The flying things were gone, and the fish things. The people remained, but they were few, and they crawled from holes in the ground. The roots which grew for them were withered and the beasts had forsaken them. And they knew not how to hunt; nor which roots are good to eat. And they wandered in bands, or alone, and they died with a terrible sickness. And hunger took them, and cold; for their robes had fallen away. And the hills echoed the cries of the lost ones, dying naked and alone.

'And their shelters were opened with the wind. And the rain fell into them and the wind blew seeds into them. Sometimes, beasts came to lie in them with their cubs and the birds made nests in them. The forest grew outside them and inside them; until their fastenings were loosed, and they fell. And the forest grew over them, and men walked over them and knew not that they were there.'

Here, the old man stopped, and seemed to be dreaming, for his eyes were blank, as if he looked on something that is far away, or long ago. And his people shuffled impatiently, because the story was not finished.

Presently Old Gart seemed to collect himself; he cleared his throat, and went on:

'The men who remained tried to continue in the old ways; but after a very long time, they forgot these ways, and learned to hunt, and to live in the forest. And the people became part of the forest, and the forest grew and was quiet.'

Somebody sighed in the shadow. It was finished.

One by one, the people slipped away. Old Gart slept now, head on chest, grey robe tight over bony shoulders; like a roosting heron.

Daf and Morg remained, gazing into the fire. The wind was cold, here, in the hills.

'They do not see, the others,' murmured Morg.

'See?' said Daf.

'The tale: that it has begun again.'

Daf rose, turning from the fire, and gazed away downhill to where the forest made a darker stain in the valley.

'They will see,' he said; and there was a great heaviness in the words. 'You sleep now: I will watch.'

And he took his spear, and went down to the wall of stones that encircled the peak.

Robert Swindells

THE GHOST MESSENGERS

Haunted by the ghosts of her grandfather and his war-time bomber crew, Meg tries to make sense of the warnings they give. The development of a neglected piece of land into a conservation area adds to her supernatural experiences, which disturb her sleep and her school work. What is the message – and will Meg be able to convince those around her of its importance?

'This well-plotted book . . . proceeds to a genuinely exciting climax.' *Junior Bookshelf*

'. . . pleasantly easy read.' *The Times Educational Supplement*

Robert Swindells

A CANDLE IN THE DARK

Sent to work down the mines as a pit-brat, Jimmy Booth enters a harsh violent world from which there seems to be no escape. Then he discovers the secret of Rawdon Pit, a dangerous secret that could change his life – or end it.